City of Beads

TONY DUNBAR

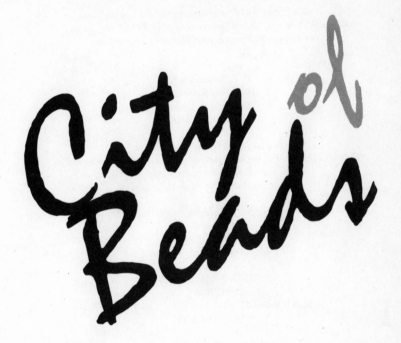

City of
Beads

G. P. PUTNAM'S SONS
New York

This book is fiction. All of the characters and settings are purely imaginary. There is no Tubby Dubonnet or Sheriff Mulé, and the real New Orleans is different from their make-believe city.

G. P. Putnam's Sons
Publishers Since 1838
200 Madison Avenue
New York, NY 10016

Library of Congress Cataloging-in-Publication Data

Dunbar, Anthony P.
City of beads / Tony Dunbar
p.   cm.
ISBN 0-399-14081-6
I. Title.
PS3554.U46336C57 1995   95-12342 CIP
813'.54—dc20

Printed in the United States of America
1   3   5   7   9   10   8   6   4   2

Book design by Jennifer Ann Daddio

Many thanks to Carrie Lee Pierson, Steven Grover, Martha Crocker, and Jon Graubarth, ingenious people who unraveled for me some of the mysteries of the computer; to Chris Pepe, my editor, Kristin Lindstrom, my agent, and Doug Magee, my friend, for their good humor; and to Linda Kravitz, Brenda Thompson, Mary Price Robinson, Anne Francis, and Philip Carter, who read my early drafts and gave all the kind advice a writer could want.

For my mother and father

City of Beads

CHAPTER

One

DOWN BY THE RIVER, POTTER AUCOIN WAS PUTTING UP A hell of a fight, but he was losing it quick.

He got in a solid clip on one of his attackers, right above the ear, with a rusty black iron jack handle. The man careened backward across the room and slammed against the wall, tipping over a filing cabinet. The other assailant, the smaller of the two but still linebacker size, leapt up behind Potter and wrapped his arms around him in a bear hug. He was blowing hot gusts of garlic into Potter's face, yelling for his partner to get off the floor and help him.

Although he was pinned, Potter managed to jab the sharp end of the jack handle into a soft part of the man holding him from behind. It dug into flesh, high on the thigh. He did it again, and a painful howl roared out of the mouth by his cheek. Potter's arms came free, but not soon enough. The beefy one on the floor, his yellow paisley tie tangled up in his blue polyester shirt, had stopped seeing stars and got up. His meaty fist was armored by an old-fashioned ring of aluminum knuckles, and it swung in a wild haymaker that landed hard on Potter's forehead. Potter's last picture of humanity was of a stranger's face, the mouth knotted in rage, before blood covered his eyes. Then the view in Potter's fading mind changed to a sandy blue seashore, and he collapsed with the taste of fresh mangoes and papayas on his tongue.

"Jesus Christ," the man with the chain-link knuckles cursed as Potter slumped down into the arms of his gasping partner, just another stranger, who held the weight for a second, then let the limp sweaty body drop to the stained concrete floor.

He stepped back with a curse, and said something like a prayer, before he gave the limp and bleeding form a tentative kick.

"I think he's dead," he said.

"Ah, no," the bigger man complained. "That shouldn't have killed him. Good God almighty, what a mess."

CHAPTER Two

TUBBY HAD TAKEN A LITTLE TIME OFF. HE HAD PICKED up some money from the Sandy Shandell case, and his current clients had no pressing problems that couldn't be solved later, so he decided to treat himself. First he talked Raisin Partlow into driving down to Florida for a couple of weeks. Tubby rented a Lincoln Town Car with a built-in CD player, stuffed the trunk full of fishing tackle and firearms, and put an Igloo full of beer, bourbon, and orange juice in the backseat. They were on their way on the afternoon of a sunny day.

Raisin played in real estate and law and mooched off his girlfriend, who was a nurse, so his schedule was flexible. On the first leg he and Tubby made it to the Flora-Bama Lounge on Perdido Key, and after hoisting a few they ended up spending the last hours of darkness snoozing in the car. They woke up at dawn and staggered down to the beach and into the crisp aqua waves of the Gulf of Mexico for a cold bracing dip. Rejuvenated and bare-chested, they proclaimed that it was good and cruised on down the arrow of beachside highway.

They caught small flounder in the surf off Pensacola, camped out in Grayton Beach, and ate flaming saganaki, souvlaki, and diples in a Greek restaurant in Tarpon Springs. They went deep-sea fishing off Sarasota, and grilled redfish and wahoo on beaches all down the coast. As they went along they rented condos by the day or weekend and tried with good humor to pick up the ladies. Tubby had a little success with a divorcée from Connecticut who was down South for the season visiting her daughter. She told Tubby affectionately that his sunburned tummy reminded her of a baby's behind. He and Raisin tossed that one back and forth all the way to Key West. It was the Sunday morning of life.

By then, however, Raisin's nurse was getting a little strident on the telephone, and Tubby had to confess to himself that he was starting to miss the stress of work. After a last round of margaritas and postcards to the girls back home they decided to turn around.

The trip back was fun, too. They stayed on the smallest roads they could find and kept to the interior, slowly traversing miles of sugarcane fields and orange groves, cruising past tiny hamlets built on patches of white sand carved out of the piney woods, and truckloads of migrant workers. Most of the faces they passed were black and stared with curiosity at the two voyagers sailing through in their hot-rod Lincoln. They bought boiled peanuts from every vendor they spied alongside the road and had important theological discussions as the miles slipped away.

NIGHTTIME ON THE NAPOLEON AVENUE WHARF, THE warm air smelled ripe with chemical decay, rich with mud and decomposing fish and insects. Long black clouds in shapes like ravens marched through the forbidding sky and held the clean breezes from the Gulf at bay. Dark and ominous, the Mississippi River expelled organic vapors and diesel fuel. It made continuous soft sounds, the water lapping at the pier and the engines of towboats plowing steadily upstream. Even the abrupt crash of train cars starting to roll was absorbed in the night.

Dull floodlamps posted high on the corners of the warehouse roof made sharp shadows out of rows of parked forklifts and turned the spaces between stacked packing crates into black alleyways.

A small building a short distance from the warehouse clung to the side of the wharf, almost hanging over the water like a tree house. Low steel barges, resembling floating shoe boxes, were lashed to the pilings below, and creaked against the timbers each time a passing ship created a little wake, or a gust of wind stirred up a wave before it died. A window, grimy and shadowed now, had been built into each end of the structure, and a plastic sign bearing the legend EXPORT PRODUCTS was nailed to the door. Loud voices came from inside. They blew over the river and disappeared. No one was around to hear them anyway.

"Shoot," the smaller man said, and he shuddered. "Well, I guess he's dead," he said again. His name was Francis, but they called him Shakes because that's what he did all the time.

The big fellow, Courtney, caught his breath and studied his metal knuckles, the blood and little bits of skin stuck to them, then bent over and wiped them off on Potter's pants leg.

"This is a screwup. No way to make this look like an accident, is there?"

"Yeah, he accidentally cracked his own head open. What are we going to do?"

"I guess the best thing to do is try to hide him." Courtney looked around the room, which was a small office furnished with a desk, some files, and piles of maps and rope and other maritime junk. Not many hideaways here. "Put out the lights. Let's look outside."

The lights went out, and the door opened slowly with a small creak. Crickets whirred from a stand of willows growing in the mud at the end of the wharf, their trunks matted with rootlets left over from high water. A hundred yards down the wharf the towering hull of an oceangoing freighter loomed above the dock, and at some distance farther along men on a floodlit crane worked at getting a massive container positioned in its hold.

"Let's just toss him in the river," the smaller man whispered.

"Hell, no. He'll float right down to the frigging French Quarter. Somebody'll see him before we even get out of here."

"Weight him down?"

"Maybe. But bodies have a way of coming right back up. Look here." He pointed at the barge tied up below. "Let's stick him in there."

"Genius at work," his partner said, and they stepped quietly back to the shed to get Potter out.

He was not hard for the two to carry, though the darkness was a handicap. They stepped clumsily over the doorsill and the rough planks of the dock. Just as they brought the body to the edge, where a steel ladder led down to the deck of the barge, a car approached slowly from behind the warehouse. The big man quickly went flat on the wharf, jerking his smaller companion down with him. Their arms linked over the dead body between them, and they got quite cozy, all but Potter.

Headlights swept over the dock, followed by a spotlight. It was the Harbor Policeman, making his rounds, eating a Popeye's chicken thigh while he looked over his dark domain, castles built of fifty-five-gallon drums, great spools of cable as thick as your wrist, crates of car parts it would take a crane to lift. He was feeling sorry for himself, thinking it was lonely out here—that there was nothing lonelier than prowling at night by yourself alone, listening to the drumbeat of your tires against the wooden planks, echoing off all that deep water. But he saw nothing out of the ordinary here. Lost in thought about scary things that could happen to a cop working solo, he drove on.

"Shit," Francis and Courtney both muttered together. They got busy again, pulling Potter to the edge of the wharf, then trying to slide him down the ladder. Finally they just let him drop the few feet onto the steel lid of the floating barge. He didn't make much noise.

It required only brute strength to roll the hatch cover back. The barge was not empty. It lay low in the water, topped with a pond of top-grade peanut oil from Georgia, refined in Cincinnati, brought down the river for shipment to Honduras as part of America's foreign aid to that country. That was the business of Export Products. Francis and Courtney had no idea what the barge held, but the big man gave out another expletive when he stuck his arm into the black hole to investigate and it came up dripping.

"Is this acid?" he gasped in a panic, looking toward the starry sky while his arm dripped all over his pants. "Good God, please let this not be acid. Let's please just get this over with."

With Francis pushing and Courtney steering, they got Potter over the open hatch and pointed downward.

"Heave-ho," Courtney whispered, and Potter slid silently into the black hold.

"Can you see him?" Francis asked.

"I never expect to see him again," Courtney said. "Let's get the hell out of here." He pulled the hatch cover shut.

Up the ladder they crept. A quick look showed no threats on the wharf, save the work crew on the distant crane, silhouetted by sodium vapor spotlights. Like mice scampering from the scene of some midnight mischief, the two jogged away, leaving behind only a trail of oily droplets.

A few moments later an engine came alive, faintly, and a pickup truck rolled out of the shadows of the warehouse, crossed the Public Belt Railroad tracks, and drove away into uptown New Orleans. The wee-hours crowd lined up outside Tipitina's to hear Marcia Ball's second set paid them no attention.

GRUBBY AND OVER THEIR LEGAL LIMITS, TUBBY AND Raisin were finally back in New Orleans. They exited the interstate on Claiborne on a weekend morning about the time the parishioners were making early Mass. Tubby dropped Raisin off at his girlfriend's house and drove off as soon as she answered the door. He did not wait to witness the joyous reception. He made it home and opened the place up. No one was there to greet him, which was just as well because he did not look his best.

There were twenty-four messages on his answering machine. He listened to them idly, sipping a last beer, ruminating on how the world kept running along even when you stepped off it for a while. The last message was only a couple of hours old. It was the hysterical voice of Edith Aucoin. Potter, her husband, had been found dead, down at the Napoleon Avenue wharf. Come right away, she cried.

CHAPTER
Three

TUBBY SHAVED QUICKLY AND PUT ON A FRESH SHIRT from his closet. He left the Town Car, with its litter of dirty laundry, maps, beer cans, and fishing rods, in the driveway and took his own car, the Corvair Spyder convertible, which he had bought on a whim when his Thunderbird's motor started knocking. The autumn morning was coming on hot, with silver clouds moving fast in the blue sky like mythical gods attacking the sun. The shocking pink crepe myrtles waved in the morning breeze as he drove down the avenue toward the river.

Potter's business was right past the railroad tracks. He had found his niche there. He brought corn oil, peanut oil, and soybean oil down the river, poured it into metal drums, and shipped it off to Mexico and Central America. The operation was really as hole-in-the-wall as you could get, especially compared to the major port activity going on all around it. The last time Tubby had visited this wharf he had seen a couple of Potter's whiskery workmen, wearing white oysterman's boots and wielding squeegees, swab the last puddle of some gray oily glop off the hull of a barge and pump it into five-gallon plastic jugs marked USDA GRADE AA.

"Does anybody, you know, strain that stuff before it goes to Mexico?" he asked Potter. He hadn't known at the time how ironic the question was.

Potter had just shrugged and scratched his chin. Whenever the Coast Guard, or anyone else from the government, passed by, he was gone. He had little use for any restraints on his God-given right of free enterprise. He saluted the flag. Potter took care of most of his business his way, with a phone in his car and a fax machine at his house.

He had gone missing about a month earlier, before Tubby had begun his Florida journey. Edith Aucoin had called Tubby and all of Potter's other friends. She said he had disappeared a couple of times before, but only for a night at a time. She was getting worried. None of them could tell her anything, so she called the police. They checked around in the desultory way they pursue missing husbands, but had no success. Tubby hadn't heard any more about it, and actually he had forgotten the whole thing until he got Edith's message on the machine. The Aucoins weren't people he saw every day.

EARLY ON A SUNDAY THERE WAS MORE ACTIVITY ON THE river than on the city streets. Tubby had to wait for a Public Belt Railway train to clank past. The brakeman hanging on the last car waved him through.

As soon as he drove through the gate in the floodwall Tubby could see the police and emergency vehicles gathered on the wharf around the Export Products shop. Only the ambulance had its flashing light on. Its two operators were sitting inside, running the engine with the windows rolled up, in a hurry to go nowhere. A Sheriff's Department car and a Harbor Police car were parked off to one side, and uniformed men lounged around both, talking quietly, in repose. The only hustle and bustle was at dockside, where some cops were working the area, measuring and observing things and taking notes. Below them, on the deck of a barge, a pair of detectives were walking around looking for whatever they could find. Seagulls trailing an upriver-bound ship hovered over their heads laughing for handouts.

One of the uniformed policemen, a young blond kid with an oversized hat, noticed Tubby.

"Can I help you?" he asked.

"My name is Tubby Dubonnet. I'm a lawyer. Potter Aucoin is my client. His wife asked me to come down."

"This is a crime investigation. You need to move away."

"Is he dead?"

"Yeah, he's dead. What is your name again, sir?"

"Who is that?" one of the detectives below called up.

"He says he's a lawyer," the policeman yelled.

"Hang onto him," said the detective, and started up the ladder. He got to the top panting.

"Put your yellow tape all around the area, and the shed," he told the officer. "We're going to have to secure it until we can pump out the whole damn barge." He turned to Tubby. "What's your interest?" he asked.

"My name's Tubby Dubonnet. I'm a lawyer and friend of the Aucoin family. His wife called and told me to come down."

"Well, she's not here. She's down at the coroner's office probably, waiting for the body."

"What happened?"

"We don't know yet, but we fished your friend out of a barge of oil."

"Did he drown?"

"Maybe. He's got some funny bruises, too."

"When did it happen?"

"We don't know yet. Something can stay fresh packed in oil a long time. Do you want to see him, Mr. Dubonnet?"

Tubby thought about that.

"I guess," he said.

The detective led Tubby to the ambulance and opened the back door.

Tubby could see the stretcher inside with a sheet covering it. The sheet was wet. The detective beckoned, and Tubby climbed inside, bending over. The two EMTs in the front seat turned around to watch but didn't say anything. Tubby pulled back the sheet, and there was the glossy face of his friend, open-eyed and serene, making a puddle on the floor.

"Peanut oil, I think," the detective said.

Tubby didn't reply. He closed his eyes and tried to collect himself. He started to pull the sheet back up neatly, but couldn't because he had to get some air. He climbed outside the van and steadied himself against the side. The day was starting to get very hot. The sound of distant thunder rolled across the river.

"Is that Potter Aucoin?" the detective asked.

"Yeah, it was," Tubby said. He was in a little swoon, aware of all the beer pitching around in his stomach.

"When did you see him last?" the detective asked, inspecting Tubby carefully.

"It's probably been two months. I've been out of town for a while."

"When did you get back?"

"Just this morning. Can we do this somewhere else? I need to go find Edith."

"Sure. You got a card or something? My name's Kronke. We can talk later."

Tubby found one in his wallet and handed it over.

"You think they'll still use the oil?" he heard one of the officers ask.

"Undoubtedly," said another. "Who's going to know."

Tubby got in his car and backed out, almost colliding with a forklift coming down the wharf.

TUBBY HAD ALWAYS LOOKED UP TO POTTER. HE HAD seemed older and wiser in some way, though he wasn't really either.

But Potter had men working for him. He moved big barges up and down the Ohio and Mississippi rivers and shipped tons of vegetable oil out of the country. Nobody else Tubby knew did that, or understood how to do it. Tubby sure didn't understand how Potter did it.

He had known Potter from college, and even then he was in business—selling T-shirts that advertised a list of "BEST BARS" on the back and featured announcements like "I Fear No Beer" on the front. Master Potter wholesaled to the bars and retailed to the students, and he still passed his courses. He organized private parties at the Lions Club hall at which the Irish Rovers or Ramblers or Renegades, Tubby couldn't remember, played, and he collected a substantial cover at the door from kids who would get carded other places. He was a great hustler, and the remarkable thing was he pulled his crazy deals off.

They lost track of each other for a few years after college. Then Potter called one day and they had lunch at Copeland's on Napoleon and St. Charles. Tubby fondly recalled the crisp little popcorn shrimp, with that tangy sauce. Potter's idea then was to get a group of inventors, innovators, and daring businessmen together to improve the city's business climate.

"The chamber of commerce is just a bunch of old guys," he said. "They don't understand that this is already the twenty-first century, and we're just part of a world economy."

"How would you know?" Tubby asked. "I didn't think you were a member of the chamber."

"I'm not, actually," Potter had to admit, "but I want to start something new. You can be our lawyer."

So Tubby had gone to the first meeting in the living room of Potter's house on Henry Clay. He took along Jason Boaz, a client of his who was the wild-haired inventor of Fruity Swizzles, with which you could stir a Coke and turn it cherry, as well as Men's Total Body Spray, which you could use to deodorize yourself from chin to toenail. Jason made big money off his ideas, in sudden spurts, then he would lose it all at the track.

Potter also had recruited a couple of others. One was a guy named Farron, who had a growing business designing T-shirts and posters with your basic New Orleans themes—jazz, booze, and seafood. Another, named Booker, owned a jazz bar where he served booze and seafood. Booker and Farron got along fine. In fact, everybody had a good time swapping stories and knocking back the drinks that Potter's wife, Edith, kept serving them. Then someone brought out a deck of cards with pictures of Earl Long on the backs, and they had to teach Farron how to play bourré. The evening ended well, though expensively, for Tubby, who dropped about $80.

The project never really developed. Tubby incorporated the Progressive Business Alliance, and Potter printed some stationery, but basically the group played cards. Potter sometimes used the stationery to write letters to the editor of the *Times-Picayune* condemning higher taxes and social welfare programs, which was a little embarrassing to Tubby.

"What's all this reactionary BS you're spouting these days?" he asked Potter once after seeing some outrageously bitter broadside in the newspaper flailing at the City for supporting a minority business forum.

Potter was insulted.

"Reactionary, hell. I'm standing up for free enterprise. The government has no business getting involved in these causes. And I'll tell you, the closer you work with the government, the more you see that scares the hell out of you."

Potter was not interested in fishing, and Tubby probably might have let him lapse as a friend if he hadn't once seen another side of Potter's nature.

Before they got divorced, Tubby's wife, Mattie, orchestrated a pretty active social life. She invited Potter and Edith over a few times for dinner, and the ladies hit it off. Potter was an entertaining guy, and he really liked the three Dubonnet girls, Debbie, Christine, and Collette. The oldest, Debbie, who was a bit of a rebellious teenager then, seemed amused by Potter's irreverent opinions about everything. For some reason, the Aucoins couldn't have children of their own.

One weekend night Debbie went out on a date with some clod named Arn, who in Tubby's opinion was way too old and shaggy but was a real catch in Debbie's eyes. She came home around eleven o'clock, and Tubby wouldn't have known anything was wrong if he hadn't been walking the family's faithful retriever and seen Potter's car drive up and park in front of his house.

Tubby strolled up just as Debbie got out, and he heard Potter say to her, "You can talk to me about this anytime."

"What's wrong?" Tubby asked, surprising them both. Debbie had left with Arn. She was not supposed to return with Potter.

"Nothing, Daddy. Mr. Aucoin just brought me home."

Tubby bent down to look at Potter behind the wheel. The face was guilty. "What became of Arn?" he asked Debbie.

"We got separated," Debbie said, avoiding his eyes. "It's no big deal. Good night, Mr. Aucoin," and she skedaddled up the walk.

"What's going on?" Tubby asked, studying Potter suspiciously.

"It would be better if she told you, Tubby. I just tried to help her out."

"Out of what?" Tubby demanded.

"Look. She's okay. It really isn't my place to tell you the story. You should talk to her about it."

Potter drove off. Tubby was mad.

Debbie was holed up in the bathroom upstairs, so he had to get Mattie out of bed, where she'd been propped up watching a late movie, and send her in to get the scoop.

She was gone about an hour, while Tubby tried to cure his frustration with J. W. Dant. The story Mattie came out with, told while she and Tubby held hands on the edge of the bed, was that Arn had taken Debbie to a bar in their neighborhood where teenagers could get served. After they hung out there for a while, Arn suggested visiting a friend of his who lived in the French Quarter. The friend sold pot and cocaine, but Debbie said she didn't know that at the time. It was an upstairs garret with a balcony overlooking an old courtyard. It felt like an adventure just climbing up the narrow dark stairs, smelling the mossy bricks and the sweet scent of night-blooming jasmine. They knocked, and Arn's friend, an older man with a full white beard, let them in and took them back to his kitchen. What a surprise to find Mr. Aucoin sitting there.

"Debbie Dubonnet," he said. "You're going home!"

He told the host that Debbie was only sixteen, the daughter of a friend of his, and they'd be leaving now.

The white-bearded man got mad at Arn, and they started arguing. While that was going on Potter took Debbie, who was completely bewildered by the scene, firmly by the elbow and escorted her downstairs and out to the street. As he steered her down the block to his car, he explained that Arn's friend sold drugs, and his apartment was no place for an underage girl to be.

She protested, but Potter got her into the car and drove her straight home. On the way he confided that he had done some drugs in the past, and he gave her various reasons why she should stay away from them. By the time they got back Uptown they were friends again, but she did wonder what had become of Arn.

"I think it was very sweet of Potter to do that," Mattie said.

"Yeah, so do I, but what the hell was *he* doing there?"

Tubby went over to see Potter the next day. It wasn't the kind of thing you discussed on the telephone. He repeated Debbie's version of events to Potter, and asked him the same question.

"I know the guy who lives there," Potter explained. "I've known him for a long time. There was a period after I got married when I was into cocaine. That's all ancient history now, thank God, but I go over to visit sometimes to replay the old days."

"Does he still deal?"

"Maybe. I mean, sure he does, but that doesn't mean I can't be his friend. It's his business, not mine."

"Then why did you make Debbie leave?"

"I knew you'd kill me if I didn't," Potter said simply.

Tubby thought about that for a minute.

"Why did you get into drugs?" he asked.

"Who knows," Potter said. "Me and Edith were having some problems. We'd just found out we couldn't have kids, and I took that kind of hard. And I was making too much money for my own good. A lot of things."

"What made you stop?"

"There's no profit in self-destruction," Potter said virtuously. "And," he added, "I suppose I like myself too much."

"Well, thanks for what you did," Tubby said. "It makes me trust you."

"Okay, but I'm a crazy, independent fool if there ever was one."

"No joke," Tubby said. "But you're all right by me."

After that he thought of Potter as someone he could rely upon, if ever the need arose.

CHAPTER

Four

THE MORGUE WAS IN THE BASEMENT OF CHARITY HOS-
pital downtown. Why are they always underground? Tubby wondered in the elevator. Because that's where you store things you
don't need? Because the dead don't require a room with a view?
The door clunked open and Tubby stepped out into a tiled hallway,
brightly lit and clinically clean. It was empty and quiet. A plastic sign
pointed down the hall to the coroner's office. He followed the arrow.

Edith Aucoin was sitting in the small waiting area between a
man and a woman who bore a distinct family resemblance to her.
The widow's unlined face was strained and her eyes were red. Her
black hair, normally loose about her shoulders, was tied back and
hidden in a purple scarf.

Tubby took the hand she offered and kissed her cheek. He
murmured how sorry he was, and she thanked him for coming. She
introduced her sister, who said they had met, and her brother, who
gave Tubby's hand a firm shake.

"Is there anything I can do?" Tubby asked.

"Just be here awhile," she said. "They told me they would be
bringing him soon."

"I stopped by the shop on the way over," Tubby told her. "The
ambulance was about ready to leave."

"Did you see him?"

"Yes, I did," Tubby said after a pause.

"How did he look?"

Tubby shrugged. "Very peaceful." Surely the crew would clean up the body before showing it to the wife.

"He would still be in that hideous barge if Broussard hadn't checked on things. I laid him off when Potter disappeared, but he still passed by the shop every so often to see if anybody was stealing stuff."

"Broussard looked inside the barge?" Tubby asked.

"Yes, I don't know why, but he did. He said he saw Potter's hair floating. And he called me from a pay phone."

"I know this is just terrible for you," Tubby said.

"He was a good man," Edith sighed, and started to weep. Her brother and sister both surrounded her with their arms.

"Yes he was," Tubby said simply. He was moved and very uncomfortable.

An attendant pushed open a swinging door and asked Mrs. Aucoin to come with him. She got up, straightened her shoulders, and walked inside with her family. Tubby remained behind in one of the red plastic chairs.

In a few minutes Edith was back. Her face was flushed and angry. She sat down hard beside Tubby and clutched his hand. Her blue eyes—gone gray—locked on his.

"Who did it?" she demanded.

"I don't know," he said.

"Will you find out for me?"

"Well, I'll sure try," Tubby said doubtfully. "I'm just a lawyer, though, Edith, not a detective. For detective work I call on pros like Sanre Flowers."

"I'm sorry. It's just all so distressing. You'll help, won't you, settle the estate and figure out what to do with the business?"

"Of course." He patted her hand.

"Thank you, Tubby. You were his friend."

After that she had to fill out some forms. The coroner passed by to express his personal sympathy. He took Edith into his office, maybe for an official purpose or perhaps to offer her a drink.

Tubby was discussing what a shame it was to the brother and sister when a newspaper reporter he knew, Kathy Jeansonne, walked into the room.

"Ah, hello, Tubby," she said, surveying him with interest, hoping she had caught him in the act of creating news. She was tall and was wearing a flannel shirt and blue jeans. She was a veteran crime reporter for the *Times-Picayune* and Tubby was not glad to see her.

"Hello, Kathy. What brings you to the basement?"

"I picked up some reports on the police radio about someone dying in a barrel of oil, and I thought there might be a story in it."

"It was a barge of oil, Kathy. Try not to get too graphic. These are the relatives."

"Oh?" She licked her lips and moved in to introduce herself. Tubby had a problem with this reporter, and it stemmed from a case long ago. She had covered his client's murder trial and reported, unfairly he thought, that his client was "wild-eyed and jittery" when he testified about the shoot-out he was accused of instigating.

"You need your contacts checked," Tubby had complained at the time. "The man was not 'wild-eyed.' He was just broken up over his poor friend who got shot."

"Yeah, like an alligator is sad when it eats its young," she retorted sarcastically.

They hadn't spoken much after that.

"Excuse me a minute, please," he said, leaving the greedy newshound alone with Edith's brother and sister. Tubby walked down the hall to the coroner's office and poked his head inside. Edith was sipping a cup of coffee, and the doctor was signing his name to some documents on his desk.

"We're just finishing up, Tubby," she said.

"Are you the lawyer for the family?" the coroner asked.

Tubby said he was.

"I'll call you after the police give me the okay and tell you the results."

"Thanks, Doctor. Could you do me a favor? We've got a reporter out here. I really don't want her pestering the family right now. Could you bring Edith's brother and sister back and show them all out of the delivery entrance, or something, while I keep her busy up front?"

"Sure, no problem," the coroner said. "We're finished here. Why don't you go and send them in?"

Tubby told Edith's relatives that the doctor wanted them. While the Aucoins were making their escape, Tubby told Ms. Jeansonne what little he knew about Potter's death and about the export business he had run before he died.

"Thanks for the background, Tubby," she said. "Why so cooperative?"

"I want to know who did it. I know you can't be beat when you put your nose to the ground."

"I'm glad you think I have some skills as a reporter."

"Just because I don't always like the way you write doesn't mean I don't think you're smart," Tubby said. Her chest expanded at the compliment.

"You want to go with me and look at where the body was found?" he asked.

"No, I'm going to wait here and talk to the widow."

"Okay, see you later," Tubby said. Good luck, he thought, and walked off down the empty hallway to the elevator back to the world.

"WHO MAY I SAY IS CALLING?" THE YOUNG LADY ASKED.

"This is Frank Mulé."

"Just a moment, sir. I'll see if I can find him."

Mulé fiddled with an extremely sharp letter opener on his desk while he waited.

"Why, hello, Sheriff," Caponata's voice boomed. "Am I in trouble?"

"You know that better than me, Joe. I just wanted to pass along a little something to you."

"Sure, what's that."

"You know Potter Aucoin, the guy who got killed?"

"No, I don't believe so," Caponata said.

"Yeah, he turned up down by the river in a vat of some kind of vegetable oil. It was in the papers."

"I might have read something about that."

"There's a lawyer, Tubby Dubonnet, interested in the case. He was down there before they even took the body away. I just thought you might want to know that."

"Never heard of him. Is he somebody to worry about?"

"It's hard to say. He pops up at the wrong times. You might want to keep an eye on him."

"Probably not, Frank, but thanks for the call."

"Anytime, Joe. Give my very best to Helen."

"Certainly. Let's have lunch."

"Maybe next week. Be my guest."

Both men hung up. Caponata brushed some cookie crumbs off his ample chest. He picked up the phone again and stuck it under his second chin. With the other hand he reached again into the cookie jar to see what was there. One thing he liked was his wife's sesame seed biscotti.

CHAPTER
Five

MIKE'S BAR WAS A FIXTURE ON ANNUNCIATION STREET, and Annunciation Street was the heart of the Irish Channel. Like the telephone poles with old campaign posters stapled to them and fire hydrants that were hooded and locked so the kids couldn't open them, Mike's was a part of the permanent background in this neighborhood, not something you noticed driving by. You'd be too busy looking out for boys on bikes and old ladies pushing Schwegmann's shopping carts around the potholes. Only regulars went to Mike's. A lot of times the door was locked and you had to get beeped inside. The only advertisement on the street was a faded gold Falstaff beer sign, swinging from a pole.

You could get lost for a spell at Mike's. The neighborhood of shotgun houses was run down now and a little bleak. It was mixed—white and black together. The parish cathedral had plywood over some of its stained-glass windows, but inside Mike's your spirits might get a lift. Today, however, Tubby was afraid it was not going to work out that way since Mike had a sad tale to tell.

Other than the mahogany bar running the length of one dim wall, the attractions of Mike's consisted of a jukebox that still played Perry Como records, three round tables, and a wall full of photographs of old politicians and little-known minor-league baseball players who had long since been put out to pasture. When holding court at the table in the back, Mike was Mr. Mike, presiding over the old-timers who kept a quiet game of bourré, pinochle, or down the river going almost around the clock, six days a week. Mr. Mike observed the Sabbath.

Walking in from the harsh light of the sidewalk Tubby had to stop a second to adjust to the darkroom lighting of Mike's. Once he could make out the major features of things he shuffled directly to the corner table to pay his respects to the owner.

"Well, if it ain't the great shyster Mr. Tubby Dubonnet," Mr. Mike said with pleasure, expelling a ball of Chesterfield smoke.

"Nice to see you, too, Mr. Mike," Tubby said, giving a squeeze to the old man's well-padded shoulder. "You're looking very handsome." There were four card players at the table, a bald man with one glass eye who greeted Tubby by nodding, a pillowy grand dame with a pile of yellow hair, who might have been his wife, a younger guy wearing a Saints cap backward, who must have been somebody's son, and Charlie Duzet, who was a criminal court judge.

"Howya doin', Judge?" Tubby said, and shook the man's thin hand.

"You got some money? You wanna play some cards?" the judge asked.

"All you need is a quarter," the lady chirped. There were perhaps thirty dollars piled in the middle of the table. "But you gotta wait for the pot to clear."

"No, he don't want to play cards," Mr. Mike said. "He wants to talk business with me for a minute. Come on, Mr. Dubonnet." He shoved back from the table, rocking it so that the young man had to grab for his beer bottle, and lifted his short round body out of the chair. "Let's go to the bar and have a conference."

He waddled to the end of the bar by the front door and with a grunt positioned his large behind on a padded stool. Tubby did likewise. The cadaverous gray-haired bartender, Larry, who never appeared to be fully awake, materialized from some shadowy spot where he roosted behind the bar and gave them each a napkin.

"You'll have what? You want an old-fashioned?" Mr. Mike asked.

"Sure, that'll be fine."

"Serve the man, Larry, and bring me a couple of cherries, too."

Larry drifted away and began concocting their drinks.

"You're doing okay, Mr. Mike? Your health is good?"

"Oh, fine, fine," Mr. Mike said, shifting his mainframe back and forth trying to find a comfortable spot. "But let me tell you what happened."

Larry set down an icy red drink in front of each of them and a small white bowl of maraschino cherries before Mr. Mike.

"Ernie ripped me off," Mr. Mike said sadly.

"Ernie?" Tubby said incredulously. "Not Ernie, your . . . partner?"

"Yes, Ernie. He was not really my partner. He was more like my prototype, or whatever. He's gone, kaput, out of town, and he took maybe fifty-five thousand dollars."

"You gotta be kidding."

"I wish I was. Not all at once. He took about twenty thousand at one pop, from upstairs. The rest he took over time. I still got Claudia looking over the books."

"Wow. I didn't know you ever kept twenty thousand dollars upstairs."

Mr. Mike gave Tubby a stare, like you've got to be kidding, and reached for the cherries.

"We used to have that much," he said. "On paydays you got to be ready for who comes through the door. We get some volume here like you wouldn't believe."

What he meant was you could cash a check at Mike's Bar, if they knew you. The bar was where lots of people banked. Only it was more interesting than a bank. The procedure was to order a drink, then slide your check over the bar to Larry in a questioning kind of way. He'd look at it, and you could swear he sniffed it, then he would slide it back to you with a pen so you could sign your name on the back. There was a mysterious little panel in the wall by the cash register, and Larry would put the check inside somewhere, and pull the panel shut. A minute or two later he would open it again and money would be there. Happy days. No ID required. It meant that now you could pay for your drink. It was bad form to count your cash at the bar, but you knew it was going to be a little short of the amount written on the check.

You could also borrow money at Mike's Bar, only it was your marker that went behind the sliding panel. Which was where Ernie had worked. Ernie the silent, the snuff spitter, the college wrestler dropped on his head once too many times. Ernie who was vaguely related to Mr. Mike and who had worked at the bar for at least ten years, closing up the place at night, escorting old folks to their cars, throwing out the occasional oaf who drank too much and peed on the floor.

"We was getting it set up where Ernie was going to take over the business from me next summer. I was going to retire. Man! I got my camp at Grand Isle fixed up real nice. All I was gonna do was fish. We were getting ready to draw up the papers. You were about to get a call. And all of a sudden the little shithead is gone."

"Are you sure it was him? I mean, it's just so hard to believe. Are you sure somebody didn't do something to Ernie?"

"That was my first thought, naturally, but it's been a week now. And he's been seen."

Mr. Mike took a healthy swallow of his drink and shook his head. Tubby waited for him to continue.

"Okay," Mr. Mike said, and wiped his chin. "He's got an aunt down in Carencro where my cousins live. And my cousin Gaspar called me. He says he saw Ernie's car behind his auntie's trailer. He didn't think nothing of it. After that he hears about my tragedy. And when he goes back over there, Ernie's car is gone and the auntie now claims she never seen him. So that's that. He's hiding out."

"It's just hard to believe."

"It hurt me deep inside." Mr. Mike patted his heart. "Ernie was like my son. Better than my son 'cause Ernie would work. There's no way I can understand why he did this to me. He was hooked on video poker, but who would have thought, fifty-five thousand dollars?"

"That's really terrible," Tubby said. "How about the money? That's got to be hard."

"You bet it's hard," Mr. Mike said. "It put a dent in my retirement, I'll tell you that. And now what am I going to do with this place? I'm too old to run it anymore. Claudia can't handle the upstairs. She wants to watch her soaps. She's in her golden years and doesn't want to be bothered counting out money all day. Besides, don't tell her, but she really ain't capable no more."

"So what are you going to do?"

"That's what I wanted to talk to you about, Tubby. You want to buy a bar?"

"What?" Tubby sat up straight.

"Seriously, Tubby. Listen to me a minute. This is a business proposition. It would be perfect for a man like you. Look around you. This is history here. . . ."

Mr. Mike continued, and Tubby ordered a second old-fashioned. The nostalgia of the place began to sink in. Mr. Mike started telling stories about who used to sit on these stools. Maybe I do want to own a bar, Tubby thought to himself. I've got some money.

"Do I get to keep all the pictures?" he asked.

CHAPTER
Six

NOT FAR FROM MIKE'S, ON A LITTLE SIDE STREET, THE Thompsons were having a family barbecue. They had the TV on the front porch tuned in to the Saints game. The home team was playing arch rival Atlanta, which always got the fans keyed up to an emotional high. Thomas and Kip Thompson were outside watching the game and keeping a grill lit in the tiny front yard, which was separated from the sidewalk by a low iron picket fence. The day was special because they were celebrating Thomas's recruitment to play baseball for the University of Southwestern Louisiana. The recruiter had promised he was going to be offered a scholarship.

They had smoked sausage and hamburgers fired up on the grill and an ice chest full of Old Milwaukee beer and Cokes. Their aunt was inside making her gumbo, soupy green and full of chicken, sausage, garlic, okra, and onions. It smelled so rich and fine that the old men in the neighborhood were starting to pass by to say hello. Their sister Tania, whose house this was, had a half-gallon bottle of Canadian Club and some ice in the living room for anybody who dropped in.

"Hurry up, Auntie," Kip called. "We're dying of hunger."

"Don't rush me," came a deep voice from inside. "It takes a long time to make things just right."

"You better get you one of these before they're all gone." Kip waved his beer can at his younger brother.

"Naw, you can do all the drinking for me," Thomas said. He was in training and so high on the possibilities stretching out be-

fore him that Kip, his beer, and even Kip's shiny Cadillac taxi
parked by the curb held no temptations at all.

Kip drove a cab for a living. That was his story, and that's what
Thomas believed. In truth, the most kindly thing Kip had ever
done was to hide from his little brother how he really made a living, which was by peddling dope.

Kip ran a string of street pushers—the kids who hung out on
the corners of even respectable neighborhoods, ready to stick their
head into any car that pulled up to make a $20 deal. This had been
Kip's thing since their father, a longshoreman on the Harmony
Street docks, slipped on a mooring cable and drowned in the river.

"Let the boy alone," Tania called from behind the screen door
where she had been listening. "He's got to keep that beautiful body
in shape for all those professional scouts when they come to watch
him play."

Nobody messed with Tania. She had been the one in charge
since their mother passed away. She had the strength of character
to see that Thomas got to school and to church. Kip was too old to
train, but she was proud of her work with Thomas.

"Go away, sister. He's big enough to be his own man," Kip
taunted.

It was halftime. All the guests were inside sampling the gumbo
and mixing drinks from the big bottle. Tania poured some potato
chips into a plastic bowl to carry outside to her brothers.

A nothing-special sky-blue car, maybe an old Ford Galaxie,
drove slowly past the house. Kip looked toward it, then jerked
around to look at his brother.

"Thomas!" he yelled.

Anything else he planned to say got lost in the noise of an auto-
matic pistol firing. Errant lead pellets broke the front windows of
the house and sent the old men and women jumping for the floor,
splashing gumbo and sweet cocktails over the walls and each other.
But several found their target and perforated Kip's chest and face,

knocking him backward onto the porch and into his sister's arms. She threw the potato chips into the front yard and fell on top of him. Thomas took a bullet in the knee. He would never look so pretty to college scouts again.

The nothing-special car didn't even speed up. It just made the corner and rolled on.

First there were the wails of the women, then the sirens came.

CHAPTER
Seven

TUBBY RECLINED UNDERNEATH AN UMBRELLA BY THE
pool in Jake LaBreau's backyard. It was a nice yard, fringed by tall
windmill palms, out by the lake.

You couldn't see the lake from the house because there was a
grass-covered levee blocking the view. The public could bicycle or
stroll along the levee and look down into people's yards, but not
Jake's because of the palm trees. The pool was a bright blue, almost
blinding under the cloudless sky, and Tubby put on his sunglasses.
He looked sharp. Jake was mixing gin and tonics at his outside bar.
A little girl, his daughter, played with an inflated giraffe in the shallow water. Both men were dressed for the occasion—tennis shorts
and colorful cotton sports shirts.

"You got a real nice place here, Jake," Tubby remarked.

"We like it." Jake brought over their drinks, pretty healthy ones
in plastic Endymion cups, sweating cold droplets. "Beth and I have
been real happy here."

He raised his glass. "To good fortune," he toasted.

They drank.

"Tubby," Jake continued, "it's been too long since I saw you.
You're staying in shape, I see." Jake settled down comfortably.
"You're getting some sun, too, huh?"

"Well, I just got back from a trip to Florida with an old buddy
of mine. We did a lot of fishing."

"That's great. I need to get away a little myself. But I've been
so busy. Beth and the little baby"—he pointed at the child splash-

ing in the pool—"get over to our condo in Destin almost every weekend, but I can't seem to get out of town."

"Your clients keep you that busy?" Jake was in the public relations and advertising business.

"I only have one client now, Tubby, didn't you know? I'm the general manager for the Casino Mall Grandé. Actually I'm more like the promotions manager. One of the guys from Vegas does the day-to-day business stuff. I just keep the machinery oiled, so to speak."

"I didn't realize that, Jake. Who's running the ad business?"

"My brother. Yeah, it's been about two months now. It was a deal I just couldn't pass up. Good steady income. Great benefits. The sky's the limit."

"I'm glad to hear it. I just never pictured you as a big-time gambler."

"The truth is, I'm not. I'm not allowed to win anything where I work, so there's no sport to it. And believe me, you don't want to go out gambling on the competitor's boat after spending all day in a casino. But it's a lively atmosphere, that's a fact." Jake took a belt out of his drink.

"I can imagine. Day and night."

"You're not kidding. But some of it is pretty mundane. And that's why I called you."

Great, Mr. Mundane, Tubby thought.

"So tell me, what can I do?"

"You know all about leases and supply contracts, employment contracts, all of that sort of thing, don't you?"

"Sure," Tubby said encouragingly.

"Well, we need a lawyer to handle all of that stuff. A lot of it is routine, or I'm sure it would seem so to a great legal mind like yours."

"Routine is okay. I'd be glad to help. Who's been doing your legal work?"

"Bacchus and Belcher. They did our licensing and got us all set up, but that's all politics. They cost an arm and a leg, too. Bacchus burps and it's two hundred bucks, but of course it's his people who do all the work. What can I say. They don't satisfy me. I can't ever get them to come to the casino. It's like they don't approve of the place. And then I thought about you."

Tubby wasn't sure if he should take offense. "I'm not exactly cheap, Jake," he said.

"Maybe not, but there ain't but one of you. I'm always paying those guys two or three at a time. And anyhow, I know you."

"That being the case, you might have yourself a lawyer."

"Fantastic. Hey, you want to take a swim, Tubby? I got some trunks in the house will fit you."

"No thanks. I'm feeling just fine." Tubby rattled the ice in his cup.

"Well then, let's go have some fun. I'll show you around the casino and give you a couple of files—mix business with pleasure."

"Dressed like this?" Tubby asked.

"Sure, dressed like that. Haven't you ever been to Casino Mall Grandé?"

"Actually, Jake, I haven't been inside a casino in ten years, and that was in Reno. I like the track. I can even stand dog races. But this whole casino thing has just passed me by. I see the crowds lined up, but I just haven't gone in."

"No time like the present, guy. Let me fix us both a go-cup and we'll cruise."

"Yeah, sure," said Tubby. Jeez, what the heck. Drink, drive, and gamble. And it was still daytime. What a way to make a living.

Tubby had definitely forgotten what a casino was like. This one took up a whole block, right in the middle of town where the tourists stay. It was along the lines of a plastic Egyptian temple. Huge columns and Sphinxes guarded its magnificent entrance. It was also very bright and loud inside, and he had the sensation of entering a giant pinball machine. Hundreds of slot machines cachunked and gonged discordantly, all jangling quarters at once, it seemed. The blackjack tables were crowded with players, regular-looking folks sitting in a half-circle surrounded by spectators, all putting away drinks. Odd noisy wheel games whirled round and round and clacked to a stop, reminding Tubby of the sound of the playing cards he had once clipped to his bicycle spokes a long time ago.

Men in evening clothes and ladies in cocktail dresses played craps, a game that he had once understood a little too well. And there were so many lovely ladies bearing gifts, trays of drinks, that you could not help pulling in your stomach. The noise level was constant, the voices happy, though surely people were losing money. Yes, here and there zombies drifted through, headed toward the doors or the bar. There were some faces looking drained and disappointed, though they didn't stay long. They moseyed on, pardner. But look at the tables. All those green, red, and black chips. Was that a hundred-dollar slot machine into whose cold metal lips the Spanish lady, looking somewhat familiar, almost could be Tubby's housekeeper, kept feeding chips?

"Whataya think?" Jake bellowed over the electronic, metallic din. "You wanna play some?"

"Not right now. I want to get the feel of the place," Tubby shouted back.

"Sure. Get the feel. Here, how about a drink. Get us a couple of gin and tonics, would you, darlin'?" he asked a waitress passing by. She smiled and marched to the bar.

"This is the world's easiest money, Tubby," Jake shouted. "It's a big damn money machine. Every day a certain amount gets bet, and we program it where a certain percentage gets won, a certain percentage gets lost, and a certain percentage flows upstairs. It operates just like a life insurance company. It's nothing more than actuarial tables. Only we don't get surprised by earthquakes or hurricanes. Nobody, but nobody, beats the odds. It's wonderful. And everybody has a good time. Thanks, doll." He smiled as she lifted the drinks she had brought and handed Tubby one. "Let me show you around."

He started wading through the crowd.

"Down here we got thirty blackjack tables, five dice, and a dozen keno, roulette, and specialty games. Back there we got six hundred slot machines. That's a lot. And upstairs we got six hundred more. Let me show you the rest."

They started upstairs. A drunk Tubby thought he recognized from his bank teetered against him on a slow-motion trip downstairs, a wild grin stuck on his face.

"'Scuse me," he said.

"Sure," Tubby replied, and gently propelled his banker on his way.

"Up here," Jake said, "we got a poker room and a bourré room. Lotsa older people come up here." A throng of settled-down ladies from across the river and old gents with their white shirtsleeves rolled up, looking as if they were in for the night, ringed the table. They were tourists in their own town, and they were having a ball.

"This is more of a family atmosphere than I remembered," Tubby said. "Or maybe it was just different in Nevada."

"Oh yeah. Listen, we're going to be offering day care in a couple of weeks. It's just a matter of seven or eight more permits," Jake said sourly. "Maybe you can help us with that. We want people to bring the kids. No sweat about finding a baby-sitter. And we're going to have entertainments for these kids like you wouldn't believe. Educational, like a miniature Disney World."

"You're making it user friendly."

"You bet," Jake said. "Come on. I'll show you my orifice, ha, ha."

Through a door marked PRIVATE they waved past a guard who pushed a buzzer that unlocked another door. Inside was the counting room, where people and machines processed quarters and bills, made them all neat and tidy, and where dozens of guys in suits walked up and down watching that things were done right.

"Look over here," Jake said.

Across a rail you could see the action below through glass panels placed above the dealers at the tables. More guys in suits monitored that action, casting a serious eye on the card shuffles and the slip and slide of chips across green felt. Others around them sat on swivel chairs, eyes fastened to television screens that tracked the progress of carts of chips and money across the gaming floors as the attendants sucked dough out of the slot machines and picked up stacks of chips from the dealers at the tables.

It was much quieter here, upstairs, than it was in the circus below. No drinks, no cigarettes or cigars, very professional.

"There's Leo Caspar," Jake said. "He's the guy who really runs the place. Let me introduce you."

From a distance Caspar wasn't very impressive. He was slender and had short black hair, a brown suit, and a narrow face that looked like it had been squeezed too hard when he was a baby. He didn't converse much as he drifted around the floor, but made little gestures that provoked reactions in employees. He was cool. When he noticed Jake and Tubby approaching, he revealed his most striking feature—hangman's eyes. Very cold, very gray, very hard.

"Leo, I want you to meet Mr. Tubby Dubonnet, Esquire. He's the lawyer I was telling you about."

Caspar checked out Tubby from head to toe. The eyes didn't like what they saw, but the lips twisted into what might have been a smile. He said, "Good to meet you," and dropped Tubby's hand.

"Mr. Caspar is our gambling czar," Jake announced exuberantly. "He's in charge of all that's glitter and gold."

"I understand that you might be doing some legal work for us, Mr. Dubonnet."

"Well, Jake just mentioned that possibility this afternoon."

"What is your legal speciality, if there is such a thing."

"Client satisfaction," Tubby said.

Caspar raised his eyebrows and looked Tubby over once again.

"In that case, we're glad to have you aboard," he said.

"I'm going to show Tubby around and let him get the feel of the place."

"Sure, go ahead." Caspar turned to Tubby. "As long as you're here, why not go downstairs and play for a while. I've got a feeling this could be your lucky night."

"I wouldn't want to clean out the house. I'd be gambling against my client."

"Don't worry about that," Caspar said. "The house can stand it. It's all simple arithmetic."

"How's that?"

"You play long enough and the house eventually wins." The eyes probed again.

"So you gotta know when to quit."

"It helps," Caspar said.

"But the winner always can come back, right, Leo?" Jake beamed.

"Generally they do. But the fact is, if you was to win enough to make a difference, we'd cut you off. I've got to go watch the count. Pleased to meet you, Mr. Dubonnet." He didn't offer to shake but nodded his head slightly, turned, and walked away. He followed a rolling safe that had been brought up from below by an attractive female attendant, flanked by two more of those men in suits.

"That's the take from one wall of quarter slots, maybe five hundred pounds of quarters. And it just keeps rolling in, Tubby. Amazing, huh? Let me show you where I work."

Jake led Tubby off to the side to a door marked MANAGER. He pressed a plastic card against a plastic square in the wall, which emitted a click, then opened the door and ushered Tubby in. It was a neat room with no windows and less character. In fact, now that you thought about it, there were no windows in the entire casino. Jake had two desks, a big rental monster against the far wall surrounded by abstract paintings and green plants, clean on top, and a smaller one, very cluttered, off to one side. A pretty blonde woman wearing a cobalt-blue dress, businesslike but on the sexy side, was sitting there, and she turned and smiled when they walked in.

"Hi, Jake," she said.

"Let me introduce you. Nicole, this is Tubby Dubonnet, a lawyer. And Tubby, this is Nicole Normande, Mr. Caspar's assistant."

They said hello and shook hands. Tubby liked the way her fingers felt. Jake mentioned that she might be seeing Tubby around because he would be doing some legal work for the casino, and she said she looked forward to that. Then Jake said why didn't she take a break and go show Tubby the tables—give him a taste of the action. And that's how Tubby found himself sitting at a $5 blackjack table touching knees and elbows with Nicole Normande.

She smelled good.

She placed a bet for him, putting a red and white chip on the table for him and another for her and talked him through a couple of hands. Tubby knew quite well how to play blackjack, but he enjoyed letting her teach him. A waitress came by offering drinks, and before long both of them were sipping rum and Coke from plastic glasses and feeling quite chipper.

"I thought there was a rule about gambling where you worked," he said.

"It doesn't apply to everyone," Nicole replied.

Tubby got into the spirit, and extracted two $20 bills from his wallet to buy four chips from the dealer, a girl who looked fifteen and whose nameplate said GISELLE. HOMETOWN: PICAYUNE, MS. She was amazingly adroit at shuffling six decks at one time.

"How ya like working here?" Tubby asked her.

"Great," she said, while she competently dealt out a hand. The other players at the table were an odd lot. To his left there was a young man with a neat black mustache, happy about a stack of $20 chips that Giselle had just shoved across to him. To his right was a small Asian woman who seemed to be betting $100 black chips exclusively. She had three tidy stacks, little missile silos, by her elbow. She kept a cigarette lit and tipped the dealer $10 every time she won. Then there was a college kid joking with his friends, and a shorthaired woman without makeup who laughed "Hah" each time she won and coughed "Hah" disgustedly each time she lost.

Nicole drew an ace and a king for blackjack, and got paid double.

"What's your strategy?" Tubby asked. His 17 won, too, when Giselle from Picayune busted.

"I don't really have a strategy," Nicole said. "But I have a system. Every third hand I double my bet."

"Does that work?"

"It seems to. Not all the time, but more often than not. I can't explain why."

"I'll see if it works for me."

It did for a while, then it didn't. After about fifteen minutes Tubby managed to lose his red and green chip at the same time and he was through.

"I'm wiped out," he said dejectedly.

"Here, let me stake you to one." Nicole placed a $20 bet for Tubby.

He drew an 18. The cards came around the table fast. The dealer had an 18, too, but when she raked up the hands and chips she pushed a red one to Tubby as if he had won. He didn't protest. Just one of those lucky errors.

Nicole was soon up to about $120 and had a very Christmassy little pile in front of her. Tubby was breaking even.

"Come on, I'll buy you supper," she said with satisfaction. "If you're hungry. I'm starved."

"Sure thing," Tubby said. He hadn't eaten since lunch.

As they got up, two people waiting behind them slid into their warm chairs. The place had gotten even more crowded since Tubby and Jake had arrived, and it took a little work just to get to the restaurant. Compared to the gaming area, it was dark and quiet.

"That was quite an experience," Tubby said, sinking back. "It's different at the racetrack. It takes a lot longer to lose when you bet on horses."

"But is it as exciting?"

"To me it's more so. I guess some people like horses, and some people like video games and flashing lights. Everybody likes being around the money."

"We've got one lady who comes in here almost every night. She is astonishing. She can put fifty quarters in a slot machine in a minute, providing she doesn't win anything."

"She must win sometimes."

"Everybody wins sometimes. But I mean she's fast. You'd think it would be physically impossible to do that."

"You ever been in a sweatshop, like down in Tijuana, where they make hand-painted souvenirs?"

"No."

"Same thing. Lightning fingers, but they're getting paid to do it."

"That sounds horrible."

"Yeah, well anyway, you ought to try the track. You might like it. It's a more serious crowd because everybody thinks they've got an angle."

"You mean the races are fixed?"

"No, but that's the atmosphere. Maybe some are fixed, like a jockey might hold his horse back to let another win, and some horse might get some kind of a pick-me-up before the race, but really, it's hard to fix ten or twelve horses and their jockeys without getting caught. Everybody just acts like they've got some kind of trick up their sleeve. The dudes who look the most shady are the kings of the track. You think they must know something. So you buy them a drink. These folks here in the casino look more like contestants on a game show. Come on down and spin the wheel."

She laughed. He liked it when she did that. A second set of creases formed and disappeared between her cheeks and lips, very deep for a moment. She stared at him directly while he mostly shot her sly glances and studied the ice cubes in his glass. She was always waiting for his eyes to catch hers when he looked up.

"You're selling people everything they want in the world of adult entertainment," he went on. "Fast action, lots of booze. And guards everywhere, so it's safe and secure. Sexy-looking people, and the theme of the show is a favorite topic, money. I need to buy some stock in this place. Let me use your phone."

"I believe you like to gamble."

"I must. I'm considering buying a bar."

"Really? Some place with video poker and lots of crowds, like this?"

"Hardly."

"What kind of place is it?"

"Just a regular bar. Guys come in to watch the game, maybe play some cards. Women come in to listen to the jukebox and hang out with people who won't give them a hard time, and see if maybe somebody'll buy them a drink. Just a regular old bar."

She looked puzzled.

"Why do you want to do that?"

"I haven't thought of the reason yet."

"I must admit," she said, "the entertainment value of this place wears off very quickly."

"I can imagine. How much time do you spend here?"

"Oh, I come in around noon and work till eight or nine o'clock. Those are the casino version of normal business hours. I try to be here whenever Mr. Caspar is, and he sleeps late."

"Oh," Tubby said.

She stared at him for a minute, then rolled her eyes and shook her head.

"I've known him for years. He was a business associate of my father's before he died."

"Oh," Tubby said again.

"He died ten years ago. He was away on business in Georgia."

"I'm very sorry to hear that," Tubby murmured. He had the strange feeling maybe she was lying.

"That's in the past."

He was happy to leave it there.

"What do you do when you're not working?" This was about as aggressive as he'd been since he got divorced.

"For fun? I like to go out in a boat, or out to the lake and lie in the sun, walk around the Quarter on Sunday, stuff like that."

"What's your attitude about fishing?" Tubby asked tentatively.

She laughed again. "I like to fish," she said. "I just don't like to clean them."

"How about Friday morning?" he asked. "I'll clean everything you catch."

"Where do you go?"

"Someplace close. Maybe Delacroix. I'd pick you up real early, and we'd go down there. We put in around sunup and go out on Bayou Boeuf. You can get an early-morning suntan. You get tired, we can come back."

"If you get me out of the city, I don't think I'll get tired."

This is great, Tubby thought.

"So we got a date then?" he asked.

"Sure, okay, we've got a date."

"I'm not kidding. Could you go as early as maybe five o'clock in the morning?"

"That's okay."

"How about four-thirty?"

"Don't push it."

"Great. Can I see you home?"

"No. I have to work here for a while. But you can write down my address."

"Sure." Tubby didn't waste any time finding a pen.

She told him it was in the 2200 block of Royal Street, in the area known as Faubourg Marigny.

DRIVING HOME PAST THE MANSIONS ON ST. CHARLES and feeling the aftershocks of his casino experience got Tubby thinking about money.

He usually didn't have much in the bank. Child support for Collette and Christine, Debbie's tuition, upkeep on his Uptown house, and a new suit here and there usually managed to soak up just about everything he collected in legal fees. True, he ate and drank quite well, but he believed that was a basic human right. In his career he had hit the jackpot only twice. The first time was an airplane crash, and his share of the check he had helped to win for the survivors had set him up in a nice office and had purchased many fine things that his ex-wife had gotten in the divorce. That's life.

There had been a long dry spell until the second time, and it had come up unexpectedly just two months before. A large sum of money, more than $300,000, had come into his hands in the course of events he still kept to himself. Not even Raisin knew about them. They involved a death never reported to the police. The good part of the story was that his client, Sandy Shandell, an exotic dancer in the French Quarter, had won twice that much as compensation for the unattractive consequences of a botched cosmetic surgery operation designed to make her skin the color of rich café au lait. When last heard from, Sandy had bought a house on Bayou St. John, invested wisely in a Merrill Lynch mutual fund, and headed off to Sweden to have his or her gender improved. And Tubby was left with a nice nest egg, even after taking care of Uncle Sam. He could leave it in the bank and enjoy the unfamiliar feeling of security.

Or he could buy a bar.

Or he could keep running off to Florida, or maybe take some trips to places his rich friends gushed about, like Montserrat or Vittoriosa, wherever the hell they were. The only problem was he didn't want to go to any of those places. To be honest about it, he didn't have anybody to go with. He found himself fantasizing about Nicole Normande. He wondered if his daughters would like her.

He drove past a two-story home on Henry Clay that had once housed a rowdy college fraternity. When Raisin was a member they dug a pit in the yard on Halloween, filled it with water and goo, and enticed students and neighborhood urchins to jump in. They were so boisterous and offensive that the university, and eventually even their national fraternal headquarters, had put the whammy on them. Tubby was thinking maybe he could buy the place, dig a mudhole, and throw wild parties—shake the block up. It was fun daydreaming about things he could do, now that he had money in the bank.

CHAPTER

TANIA THOMPSON HAD BEEN WAITING ALMOST MOTION-less in the front seat of her car for nearly an hour. Every so often her toe would get loose and tap itself against the brake pedal, but she would calmly tell it to stop. Be a part of the wall, she reminded herself, even though there was no wall on this particular street. That was what she had successfully done for most of her life, but here it was no simple matter. Women didn't sit by themselves in parked cars on Persephonie Street after nightfall. People in this neighborhood of pretty Victorian homes, built close together like petit fours in a gift box, separated by tall hedges and bamboo, sat indoors at night. They didn't stay in their cars keeping their eyes on a quiet two-story house with green shutters.

There was even less of a reason for an African-American lady to be there, on this particular block. Lucky she was hard to see. It was after eight o'clock at night, and Tania's parking place was shielded from the distant street lamp by overhanging tree branches. She was a small person and hoped she blended into the shadow of her seat.

A man and a woman passed by, walking their dog. She heard a fragment of their conversation.

"Her dress was slit way up her thigh," the man said, but they did not notice Tania. She was used to that.

Tania was studying about a problem, which was how to kill Charlie Van Dyne. It was not an easy question because Charlie Van Dyne was a careful man and surely well guarded. He was powerful, and she was small potatoes. But she approached it analytically and optimistically, which was her nature. Tania had learned a lot of practical survival skills in her thirty-one years. Though she had never left the Irish Channel where her mother had raised her, she had grown up to be a branch manager for First Alluvial National Bank. She had not worked herself into that position on her good looks, though she was very pretty, and prim like a schoolteacher. She was just a competent manager and could make her boss look good.

You solved problems, she knew, by thinking them through, by keeping your cool. Holding your reactions under control. Quite a talent to have when you had seen your own baby brother nearly chopped in half, until that moment having a good time watching the Saints game on her front porch with the whole family hanging around, by 9 millimeter bullets spat out from some gun that when the police named it sounded like a kind of computer or foreign car.

Tania had been coming out the front door, bringing chips and dip, when the car drove by and her brother began howling and spouting blood all over the shiny white siding of the house. Somehow she didn't remember hearing any shots, but she remembered the excited, serious face of the man leaning out the car window with his gun on fire. She didn't know the man, but it was the same ugly, nameless, violent face she had secretly been afraid of all her life.

At the hospital, then the police station, then the wake, she heard several possible gunslingers mentioned. Her brother Kip had been dealing drugs on the street. Tania had known that for a long time. She thought he had quit, but she had just been misled by his bullshit and her affection for him. From various relatives and friends of Kip's she picked up clues to the identity of her brother's assassins, names like Coco and Hambone, and for the first time she heard the name Charlie Van Dyne. That name wasn't mentioned to the police, but her brother's grieving widow, Charmaine, damned

Charlie Van Dyne from the lonely privacy of her tiny living room, accusing him of being the boss who ran things, or at least the boss that Kip knew about. It was Van Dyne or someone higher whom Kip had offended, and he had ordered her man killed.

Tania thought about her loss, the injustice of it, almost all the time. Even when she was carrying out her duties at the bank she dwelt upon it. The police had made no discernable progress. In fact, they seemed to lose all interest after the first day. Just one more drive-by shooting, one more horrible homicide in what was shaping up to be a record year in the Big Bad Easy.

"This city is a dangerous place." That's what the police detective had told her when she had last called to see if they were getting closer to arresting anybody.

"People think New Orleans is just Mardi Gras beads and Bourbon Street, but there's a world of hurt out there, too. I don't have to tell you," the policeman said sadly.

She knew all about that hurt. The unsolved crime insulted her sense of rightness, and she stayed awake at night, unable to fit it into her life.

She wished all sorts of evil on Coco and Hambone. They came to her in nightmares. Tania prayed almost constantly about what to do.

Finally, one Sunday morning during services at the church in the neighborhood where she had always gone and where they called her Sister Thompson, a peaceful sensation washed over her in the middle of the preacher's sermon. Her muscles relaxed and the creases disappeared from her forehead. She exhaled a great gust of anger and it was gone. In no more time than it took to inhale again, she was able to forgive Coco and Hambone. They were God's children, too, and God's business. They would haunt her dreams nevermore. Charlie Van Dyne, on the other hand, was her personal responsibility. He was beyond the reach of the law, and he deserved to die.

There was no Charlie Van Dyne in the phone book, however. According to her sister-in-law, Van Dyne lived somewhere uptown off Jefferson Avenue. At least that's what Charmaine recalled Kip saying. On her lunch break, Tania went to the public library and studied the city directory. Every house in the whole city was listed by house number, as well as the name of the person who lived there. She checked the addresses on Jefferson from the river to Tonti Street, but no Van Dyne was to be found. Tania kept at it, and she finally discovered one R. C. Van Dyne on Persephonie Street, just a few blocks from Jefferson.

The next night after work, and after she had eaten a light supper, Tania drove up and down Persephonie until she found the address. The house was hidden behind a tall hedge but you could see it was well lit up. A semicircular driveway permitted direct entry into the front door from a car.

Tania parked where she could watch the door. A compact black Cadillac sat empty in the driveway. Barely had she cut off her engine, however, when two men in loud suits came outside. One opened the passenger-side door for the other, let him in, then came around and got behind the wheel. The Cadillac started, headlights came on, and it swung around the driveway suddenly, its lights sweeping over Tania. She was too surprised to do anything but stare straight ahead. The Cadillac accelerated up the street. Tania got her own mind working quickly, and pulled out to follow.

Assuming that Van Dyne was the passenger, she now knew that he was handsome, tall, and strong-looking. She followed the Cadillac to Derbigny Street, then across Tulane to Mid-City. It pulled into the dim parking lot of the Bouligny Steak House, and Tania, from across the street, watched the two men get out and go into the neon-lit restaurant.

Tania parked outside under the streetlights for almost an hour and a half. A panhandler spotted her and tried to engage her in conversation, but she refused to open the car window. After tapping on the glass and making a face he went away. To occupy herself she went over the day's events, thought about a customer who had complained about one of her tellers, and wondered where she would get a gun.

Finally the two men came outside again, laughing. Charlie paused to light a cigarette. Then he was let back into the Cadillac. They drove away, and Tania followed them back uptown to Persephonie Street. The car entered the driveway, and the men got out and went back inside the house. She maintained her vigil outside until almost eleven o'clock. When she caught herself falling asleep, she decided to go home.

She repeated much the same program on the following two nights, and Charlie's routine stayed constant, except that he went to Ruth's Chris one night and Pascal's Manale the next. He was a very satisfied-looking man.

A plan began to form in Tania's mind. It was nothing complicated, because she had learned in her professional life that the simplest approach was the one most likely to succeed. And she remembered where to get a gun. Her brother Kip had had one. He kept it in the table beside his bed. Tania went calling on the widow Charmaine that evening after supper, and, when she was left alone for a minute, she found the pistol and furtively put it in her pocketbook. Things were falling into place, and she went to bed that night eager to wake up and face the day.

Her boss came by her desk and complimented her.

"How have you been?" he asked.

"Busy," she said with a smile.

"You know I always think you do a good job, Tania, but lately I've thought you're putting out some real extra effort, like you are enjoying your work."

"Why, thank you, Jerry," she said.

"I just wanted you to know I noticed," Jerry said.

CHAPTER
Nine

ON THE DAY FOLLOWING TUBBY'S RETURN FROM FLOR-
ida, after he had made his visit to the morgue, slept and washed the
stars out of his eyes, he had called up his oldest daughter, Debbie,
to invite her out for a meal. It took them about a week to get together. They met for an early supper at Crêpe Nanou uptown, a favorite of hers. He ordered crabmeat crêpes, and he had to admit
that, though real men had trouble pronouncing "crêpe," they
weren't bad. The spicy mixture wrapped in a light pancake was
quite tasty. Debbie liked sweets, and tonight she had crêpes with
sour cream and peaches. She dug in while he told her about
Florida, and seemed to enjoy her choice immensely.

"It sounds like the two of you had a lot of man-fun," she said,
smirking as if she knew what that was.

"That about sums it up," Tubby said. "Much more fun and we
couldn't have made it back."

"Did Raisin have a good time?"

"The best."

"Doesn't he have a girlfriend now?" Debbie always seemed interested in Raisin. A lot of people did. How did he get away without ever having a steady job? How the hell did he pull it off?
Seeing him any day of the week looking fit on the tennis courts at
Tulane or the club on Jefferson Avenue was enough to make accountants and doctors shake their heads in wonder. Tubby knew
Raisin's secret. Don't worry. Be happy. Just say No.

"Yeah. Melinda. She's a nurse at Hotel Dieu."

"She must be very tolerant," Debbie pried.

"It's hard to say." Tubby tried to be noncommittal about Raisin, the reason being he'd known the guy for over twenty years and still couldn't predict what he'd do next. No doubt this was the feature that attracted more than a few women to Raisin—even those in the pre-geriatric set they were starting to run with.

"But you had a terrible homecoming." She sat back and pushed aside her plate on which she had abandoned a tiny crisp of her supper. "What an awful way to die." Debbie had inherited bluntness from her mother.

"They think he was dead before he was dropped in the oil, but anyhow you're right. It sure isn't like dying at home in your sleep. Potter was a good guy. We had some real nice times together."

"Do you remember the time Mr. Aucoin brought me home from the French Quarter?" she asked.

"I sure do. I respected him for that."

"I guess I do, too, now," she laughed. "He really said some things that made me think a lot about drugs."

"Whatever happened to your date from that night?" Tubby asked.

"Arn? He got married. He's studying art at UNO and living with her parents. He turned out to be a jerk."

Tubby nodded, his judgment about boyfriends again confirmed.

"Mrs. Aucoin, she must be in shock."

"Actually she's coping pretty well," Tubby said, patting his lips with a napkin. "She was down at the morgue when I got there. Dr. Jazz came by to pay his respects. She was calm and went home with her brother and sister. She was great at the funeral, making all the people feel better. I called her today about the estate and everything. I don't think it's completely hit her yet."

"What do the police say?" she asked.

Tubby waved the waiter over and ordered coffee. What kind of dessert did you have at a crêpe restaurant? Maybe they could go someplace else.

"They're still looking for some kind of motive. There's not a whole lot to steal in a shipping office, especially not the kind of popgun operation Potter ran. And the cops haven't the slightest clue as to what his business was about, so they can't really investigate that too much. But really, who steals peanut oil? Their first thought was maybe he fell in the hold of that barge all by himself, but that was a dumb idea. Potter wouldn't even step on his barges 'cause he didn't like to get dirty. Anyway, the coroner nipped that since there was a head wound nobody could miss. I don't think they have any leads at all. Except for the fact that Potter knew a couple of important people, like from card games, they wouldn't even be going through the motions."

"Can you do something?"

"Hey, I'm not a sleuth. I'm a lawyer."

"Yo" was all Debbie had to say to that. She sipped her coffee. "I wish you would help me with a legal problem, Daddy."

Tubby was immediately alarmed. "What's the trouble, honey? Of course I'll help."

"Oh, not me," she said quickly. "It's this group at school, Save Our River. They've been trying to find a volunteer lawyer to file a case against some polluters."

"Well, let's see. I don't know anything about environmental law," Tubby hedged. "Don't they have a law clinic at Tulane for that sort of thing?"

"Yes they do, Daddy, but they've run out of money or something. They're not taking on any new cases right now."

"I didn't know you were involved in environmental work. Is it some kind of club or something?"

"It's a real organization," she said defensively. "It's mostly people from school, but they have members from all over."

"Tell me more about it. When did you get involved?"

"I've been going to meetings for a couple of weeks. Marcos took me to one. His roommate's the chairman."

Oh, that explained things. Marcos was a boyfriend. He was a permanent student, on sabbatical from his family estates in Mexico, with an interest in biology. He was good-looking, well off, always polite, spoke English beautifully, and Tubby was running out of reasons not to approve of him.

"The main objectives," Debbie continued, "are to get the river cleaned up and to catch the major polluters."

"That's kind of hard," Tubby said, "since we are at the tail end of a two-thousand-mile open drainage ditch that starts in garden spots like Pittsburgh and the copper mines of Butte, Montana. And along whose shores any ship or barge that wants to can just flush its hold and send a highly toxic surge toward New Orleans. How are you going to police that?"

"You have to try, don't you? A lot of that chemical waste comes from right here, so we're responsible. For goodness sakes, we drink that stuff."

Shocking, but true. Over the levee at Oak Street, there they were. Big pipes sucking in the brown muck of the river, happy with fish and swirling with an occasional rainbow, all pumped into the treatment plant. There it was given a rest, laced with chlorine, treated to sunshine, and sent out to fertilize the populace. Those who could afford it drank bottled water from some less urban aquifer up north, or drank wine.

"It's a big problem, to be sure," Tubby hemmed.

"Couldn't you help, Daddy? I know you're busy, but I bet you could make a big difference."

Actually he was not very busy. If he didn't get motivated he was going to find himself without any clients.

"What do I have to do?" he asked.

"Just be a lawyer. I'll tell Twink Beekman. He's the president. I don't know the details of the case since I just joined the group. I've only been to one meeting actually, and I heard them say they needed lawyers. I'm sure he'll call you soon."

"I'm sure he will, too," Tubby said. "Are you finished?"

"Yes. It's time I was getting back to my apartment. I have to study."

"No dessert?" he asked mournfully.

"Oh no, I couldn't. But I'll sit here if you'd like to have some."

"No, I guess not." Tubby patted his stomach virtuously.

He paid up and drove Debbie back to her new apartment on Hampson Street, the one she shared with two other girls.

"Thanks a lot for dinner, Daddy," she said when she got out. "And thanks for offering to help save the river. And, oh, I'm so sorry about Mr. Aucoin." She shuddered and was gone. He watched her get inside the door, then drove away cautiously, the street made narrower by all the students' Jeeps and Japanese cars parked along both grassy curbs.

THE MYSTERY OF POTTER AUCOIN'S DEATH TOOK AN IN-teresting twist the next morning. Kathy Jeansonne, the newspaper reporter, called.

"You're a real butt," she said, by way of hello.

"What are you talking about?"

"Real cute, ditching me at the morgue."

"You writers always talk that way?"

"I watched two more stiffs get wheeled in before I figured out the Aucoins weren't coming back."

"You'll probably get some good stories out of it."

"Sure, watch for my byline."

She asked Tubby if he knew anything about the Aucoin drug connection. He wanted to know what she was talking about.

"Did you know the police found a package containing more than a quarter-pound of cocaine in his office?"

"No." Tubby couldn't believe it.

"That's right. They're keeping it a secret, but not from me. So how do you think this figures into the murder?"

"I don't know. It's news to me. If Potter was shipping drugs I'd be shocked."

"And wild-eyed, no doubt," she said, unable to resist a dig.

"Yeah, well, thanks for calling me."

After she hung up, he conceded that it might be true, considering what he knew about Potter's past. Maybe you never could really give up cocaine once you started. Maybe the lure of big money had just been too strong for Potter.

But he hadn't seen any indicators that Potter desperately needed cash. They had sent the books over to a CPA, Jerry Molideau, to review, and the preliminary report was that the company had good funds in the bank. Tubby had collected the legal documents from Edith, who got them out of her safe-deposit box, and they showed that Export Products had leased its spot on the wharf from the New Orleans Levee Board, that the company had options to renew running fifteen more years, and that the rent was current.

Edith had put Broussard back to work processing the last of the oil shipments Potter had secured. With the boss gone, no new contracts were being bid. Broussard was shutting things down. It stood to reason that if the police had found drugs in a dead man's office they would be checking the barges that were still passing through. And if they had found anything big, there would no longer be a secret about drugs. Edith would at least have been questioned. The whole thing didn't make sense, but it raised disappointing questions about Potter.

CHAPTER Ten

TANIA HAD THE GUN IN HER PURSE WHEN SHE STALKED Charlie Van Dyne on Tuesday and again on Wednesday night. She lacked confidence in her aim, since the only weapons training she had had was watching cop shows on television. There was no way that, seated in her car, she could hit the man when he came out of his front door, and she could not even picture herself hiding in a hedge and running across a lawn with a pistol in her hands. So she would get him at a restaurant.

On Tuesday night, however, he set off in a new direction and ended up at Clancy's, which had valet parking. On Wednesday he went to the Upperline, which paid an off-duty policeman to hang around on the street.

But on Thursday she followed the Cadillac back to Derbigny Street and eventually back to the Bouligny Steak House. This historic establishment served one of the largest porterhouses in town, but the place was so old that almost all of its customers had died. It hadn't yet been discovered by a young crowd so it was the perfect choice for an intimate meal. Like nobody else might be there. And if you really wanted isolation you could eat in a curtained booth. On this night neither valet nor lawman was visible in the parking lot.

Only one other car, maybe the cook's, was there when the Cadillac pulled in. Both men got out at the same time. Tania watched from across the street, as she had once before. After half an hour of smelling beef grilling in the distance she started up, made a U-turn, and got closer. She slowly entered the lot and took the exact spot next to the Cadillac, on the passenger side. She switched off her lights. Except for the two other cars, the place was deserted. She got the .38 revolver out of her purse and warmed it up in her lap. It was fully loaded and the safety was off. She had checked those things a dozen times. It really took no genius to operate a handgun. If you didn't believe that, it was time for you to wake up and smell the coffee. That's the way Dear Abby put it, and Tania read Dear Abby every morning at her breakfast table at her house.

She thought about other remarkable advice Abby had given to other troubled people, pregnant girls and women whose husbands snored, over all those years. Thus her mind stayed occupied while she waited for Charlie Van Dyne to finish his steak.

Abby was like Tania, caring but capable. Practical. Problems were to be confronted and handled. You did your best. A panicky doubt passed over her just then, that killing the man was the wrong thing to do. The feeling had come before, and she erased it in a second. What she was about to do was necessary for her well-being, it was that simple. It was fair, and it would make the world a better place. Thank you, Dear Abby.

Voices came suddenly from the front of the restaurant, and she saw Charlie Van Dyne and his manservant round the corner. They paused, as she had seen them do before, while Charlie fished out his cigarette and his bodyguard found a match.

They said something to each other and Charlie shrugged. The driver started to come around the car to the passenger side, but Charlie mumbled, "That's all right," and the man changed course toward his own door. Charlie walked past the headlights of his own car and waited, just a few inches from Tania, while his driver got in and popped up the door locks. Charlie opened his door and stooped to get in.

He had taken no notice of Tania, but now she quickly rolled down her window.

"Mister," she said softly.

Charlie was in the car now, in his seat with his hand on the door to pull it closed. He was startled by her voice and looked at her with questions in his eyes.

"Do you have a light?" she asked sweetly.

Charlie turned away to get the lighter from his driver, and when he turned back Tania had the pistol pointed out the window right in his face.

"Whoa," Charlie said.

Tania hissed like a cat, and with both hands tight around the butt she pulled the trigger with all her strength.

Charlie's forehead split apart, and he slammed back against his driver. The inside of the car was littered with gore.

"Jesus Christ, lady!" the driver cried, moving his terrified eyes back and forth from Tania's and her gun. His face was speckled with organic matter, and he had involuntarily hugged Charlie's body against his own as a shield. What remained of Charlie's head rested wetly against his shoulder.

Tania didn't want to kill the bodyguard. He was not a part of the justice equation.

"You stay where you are, all right?"

"All right, lady. Jesus," the man said, pulling Charlie closer to him. Tania put her gun back in her lap and started the car. She backed up fast. As she left the lot she saw the front door of the restaurant open a crack and a head poke out, a cautious investigator. Then she was gone.

Her mind raced ahead of her all the way home, replaying the event again and again, while some attentive mass of cells remembered to tell her to stop at red lights, to find Laurel Street, and to park by her house.

She got inside and locked the door behind her. She went to the cupboard where there was a dusty bottle of Canadian Club left over from Kip's last party, and she poured herself a drink. Once she sat down and tasted the alcohol she began shaking uncontrollably. It lasted about a minute, during which she whispered a rambling prayer to God. And the peace came to her.

She sighed and finished her drink. She picked up the pistol where she had dropped it by the front door in her haste and carried it into the kitchen. Pulling a nearly full garbage bag out of its plastic can, she thrust the pistol, cartridges and all, wrist deep into the trash. Then she tied the bag and dragged it outside to the street. Tomorrow was garbage day. In the morning it would be gone.

CHAPTER
Eleven

TUBBY MET ADRIAN, BETTER KNOWN AS MONSTER MUD-bug, in the cathedral-ceilinged hallway of the Criminal District Court, Section T, at Tulane and Broad. Adrian was very happy to see him, and he jumped up with his hands waving. He was nervous. He had been worried that his lawyer wouldn't arrive, even though Tubby had faithfully appeared the last half dozen times Adrian had been in a jam.

"Mr. Tubby, it's real good to see you, yes sir." He grabbed Tubby's hand and shook it.

"All right, Adrian, how're you making it today?"

"Not so good. I don't want to be here, that's for sure."

"This shouldn't take too long. Have you got some paperwork with you?"

"Yeah. Here's what I got. I'm sorry it's kind of crumpled."

From the back pocket of his jeans he produced a blue Notice to Appear and a wrinkled receipt from a bail bondsman.

"You gave the bondsman twenty-five hundred dollars cash for a twenty-five-thousand-dollar bond?" the lawyer asked, translating the faded carbon copy.

"Right. My dad came down with the money to get me out of Central Lockup. I'm going to pay him back."

"Okay, you're charged with theft of a movable. Car theft?" Tubby knew nothing about the case. He had just gotten a message from Adrian's father telling him his son was messed up again and what court he was in.

"A motorcycle. Ain't that a trip?"

"What happened?"

"I don't even know." Adrian shook his head like he was trying to clear the sawdust out of it.

"Well, bear down a little on this one, Adrian. Real quick now. They're going to call the docket in just a minute. Tell me what you do know."

"Okay. I'm down at Bennie's Bar, listening to music. We're all drinking. I'm out of it. I mean totally out of it. And these guys tell me their motorcycle won't start, or something. So I help them put it in the back of my truck, and then whoop, whoop."

"Whoop, whoop?"

"The cops show up and we all get arrested."

"It wasn't these guys' motorcycle?"

"I don't think so."

"Who are these guys?"

"I don't even know their names."

"They got arrested with you?"

"Yeah, I think they're still in jail."

"Where did you think you were taking the motorcycle?"

"I don't know. To the guys' house or something. They couldn't get it started was the story. I'd had quite a few beers."

"How'd you get it in the truck?"

Adrian made a motion to show he had lifted it. He was a towtruck driver, and he was seriously muscular, like he worked out with weights.

Tubby massaged his forehead and looked at Adrian through his fingers.

"You're in a real tough spot, Adrian. I can't sugarcoat that. This isn't like a traffic ticket or something. It's a major charge. Let's see if we can get you out of it." He guided his client through the tall doors into the courtroom. The benches were filling up, and there was considerable activity among the clerks surrounding the judge's bench. Several prisoners from the jail wearing orange jumpsuits were led in, shackled, and put in the jury box. The judge might not take the bench for an hour, during which time a great many matters would have already been disposed of. Tubby hoped Adrian's would be one of them.

"Have you ever been arrested before, Adrian?" Tubby asked as they pushed into the throng.

"You know me, Mr. Tubby."

"No, I don't mean for traffic offenses." Tubby knew all about those. Adrian had been stopped numerous times for piloting his Monster Mudbug float, known as the Rolling Boiler, down public thoroughfares without benefit of a parade.

"Sort of," Adrian admitted, worried.

"What for?"

"There's the DWI, and my ex-wife had the cops talk to me once for coming around to see my kid."

"But nothing like stealing something? Nothing like with a gun?"

"No way, Mr. Tubby."

"Okay, you sit here."

He planted Adrian on a crowded pew in the back and made his way forward through the swinging gates that separated those who were part of the system from those who were not.

He stopped to chat a minute with the clerk, located Adrian's file in the pile on the table, and with a sober look carried it through a door behind the judge's bench. There were already two other lawyers waiting to see the assistant district attorney, outside a tiny room used for that purpose. Tubby didn't really know the other attorneys, but he recognized their faces.

"How's it going?" he said to one and all.

"Same ol', same ol'," the man in front of him grunted in response. A couple of the others nodded.

"Mr. Dubonnet," the lucky guy at the head of the line said. "I

know you don't remember me, but I was in your class on trial tech-
niques three years ago at Loyola. Johnny Rolland."

"Sure, Johnny. I remember," Tubby said, shaking his hand.
"You doing everything we taught you?"

"Trying to, and here we go."

The door to the inner sanctum opened. A lawyer clutching a
briefcase came quickly out, and she gave a secret smile to the line
as she passed. Johnny Rolland slipped inside and said, "Good
morning, Mr. Pettibone," loudly as he closed the door.

"The DA's name is Pettibone?" Tubby asked the man in front
of him.

"Yeah. He's easy to deal with. Just doesn't like drug dealers
though."

Tubby leaned against the wall and relaxed. His client wasn't a
drug dealer. The picture of Potter Aucoin's body came back to him.
He tried to shake it off, but it wouldn't leave. Why would anybody
kill Potter?

Rolland came out.

"Piece of cake," he whispered to Tubby as he squeezed past.
The next man went in, and Tubby was on deck.

He looked at Adrian's trial notice again. What a stupid way to
get busted.

The door opened. The lawyer emerging said, "Thanks a lot,
Joe," and held the door for Tubby.

"Good morning," Tubby said.

The assistant DA was an extremely underweight black man
with neatly clipped hair. It was obvious that he was tall, since his
knees could barely squeeze under the small metal desk he was sitting behind. There was a chair next to him, but no other furnish-
ings. It was worse than an interrogation room at the police station.

"What can I do for you?" Pettibone asked, without much interest.

"I'm Tubby Dubonnet, Mr. Pettibone, and I'm here to see you

about Adrian, or Monster Mudbug." He handed the file to the district attorney, expecting to get a smile.

The man did not oblige. He took the folder, but did not open it.

"I'm familiar with the case," he said.

"Then you know that my guy was just an innocent bystander. He's actually kind of a babe-in-the-woods. I'm sure you've seen him in costume at Mardi Gras, Monster Mudbug?"

Pettibone made no comment.

"Anyway, he thought he was just helping some fellows whose motorcycle broke down. He had no idea they were stealing it."

"Tough luck for him," Pettibone said.

"Well," said Tubby, "it was just a mistake. He wasn't trying to steal anything."

"That's his story."

"Yes, and it makes sense. He doesn't have any record. He's employed full-time as a towtruck driver. He's a well-known public figure. He's got no need to steal a motorcycle."

"He was caught in the act. Who knows why people do things?"

"This guy is innocent, Mr. Pettibone. Can we do anything here today?"

"If he'll plead guilty to first-degree theft, seeing it's his first offense, the judge might put him on probation for three years."

"That's no deal at all. He's not guilty, except of being stupid."

"Let's go to trial."

"How about agreeing to a bail reduction. He's working steady. How about we release him on his own recognizance."

"I'm not agreeing to any such thing. You can always take it up with the judge. He might do it. I don't know."

"How about reducing it to five thousand?"

"No, Mr. Dubonnet. I'm not going to agree to cut your client any slack." Pettibone slapped his hand on the table. "I've talked to the arresting officer. He wants to make the case. I'm agreeable. So let's go to trial."

Tubby couldn't think of anything else to say. The old charm was about tapped out. He had been completely shut out before, but it had been a long time ago.

"Okay. See you down the road." He got up and left.

"Piece of cake," he muttered to the next lawyer waiting in line.

On the way out he said a few more words to the docket clerk and got the case continued for two weeks. Tubby was suddenly very tired of being a lawyer. He wasn't at all sure he wanted to keep doing this.

Adrian was fidgeting in his seat at the back of the courtroom. Tubby walked right past him, so Adrian jumped up and followed him out into the hall. He could tell by the look on Tubby's face that things were less than perfect.

Tubby stopped outside and leaned against the marble wall. He thought about how this would be a good time to light a cigarette if he still smoked.

"So what happened?" Adrian asked.

"Is there something you haven't told me about this thing?" Tubby demanded.

"No, I don't even remember getting arrested."

"This guy back there has a super hard-on for you. The best he'll do is let you plead guilty and get three years' probation."

"Plead guilty? I'd never get to see my kid again. That's a terrible idea."

"I know, but right now you're in big trouble. They've set it for trial early next month. I can try to talk to the other guys who got busted with you to see if they will tell what really happened."

"Gosh. No telling what they'll say. I don't even know their names."

"I can find that out. Now listen, I need a retainer for this of two thousand dollars."

"Gosh, Mr. Tubby, I don't have that much right now. My rent is due and everything."

"Adrian, I'm not going to lead you astray. During those times in your life when you've got serious legal troubles, I suggest you pay your lawyer before you pay your rent. You could try out another lawyer, and it wouldn't hurt my feelings one bit. But you gotta expect to lay out some money when you get yourself in a fix like this. I'm giving you some good advice here."

Adrian hung his head down and thought it over. "I guess I've got only myself to blame," he said. "I'll talk to my dad about borrowing some more money."

"Whatever. But get in touch with me soon while we can still locate your partners in crime."

They left together. Tubby offered Adrian a lift downtown, but he said he would be better off walking to Canal Street and catching a Cemetaries bus back to his house. Tubby's Corvair was in the other direction. It was unsafe at any speed and matched his mood exactly. He marched down the sidewalk feeling frustrated, angry, and tired.

THE PRALINE LADY WAS SITTING WHERE HE HAD LAST seen her, on a folding lawn chair, on the sidewalk, across the street from the Community Correctional Center. She had on a straw bonnet, held down with a red-checkered scarf, and a light pink raincoat buttoned up despite the warmth of the day. She was as out of place, displayed against the white concrete walls of the prison, as a potted geranium would be on the beach.

On her lap there was a cardboard box top on which were arranged nice round pecan pralines. Tubby spied her from the car and he detoured to see how she was doing.

"They look good today," he said. She jumped a little.

"Dear me," she peeped. "I must have fallen asleep."

"I'm mighty sorry to wake you up," Tubby said, "but I was hungry."

"You just pick out whichever one you like." She lifted the box top so he could see better. Each of the saucer-shaped confections was wrapped in its own little bag, tied with a red twist.

"This one looks good," Tubby said, selecting the biggest one he could find. He handed over a dollar bill. "You don't remember me, do you?"

"I remember you," she said with a small sly smile. "You the one asked about my godson, Jerome."

"Yes. Jerome Rasheed Cook. Has he ever come out of there?" Tubby indicated the doorway to the prison complex.

"No, he ain't," she said accusingly. "And I been watching for him every day."

"You know, I asked the guard to give him my card the last time I was down here, but I never did hear from your godson."

"They probably never give it to him. He would have got in touch with you if they had let him. There's something they don't want you to know going on in there."

"Maybe." Tubby unwrapped his candy and took a sweet bite. "It is strange. You know, they had him on the computer, but they couldn't tell me what he was charged with when I was here last time. I don't know what it means."

"Police arrested him for selling that crack. Say he was a witness. They wanted him to say who he got it from."

"He wouldn't tell?"

"He told me," she said, a crafty look upon her weathered brown face.

"What did he say?"

"Oh, I wouldn't repeat that."

"That's probably smart. He should do the telling. But the question is, where is he? Haven't you gotten a letter from him in all this time?"

"No, not one single card," she said emphatically, patting her hand on her knee.

"Well, look. Something's not right here. If you want me to look into this I will." It might make him feel better about screwing up Adrian's case.

"I'd be mighty happy if you would."

"Well, you've got to hire me. I'll take another praline as a retainer."

She squinted up at him, trying to decide if he was worth that much. "That's all you want?" she asked.

"For now," Tubby said. "If it gets involved, we'll have to talk some more."

"I don't know about that," she said, "but I'll pay you one praline for today."

"That one there," Tubby said.

She handed it over.

He walked across the street to the prison and, as he had done before, presented himself to the black-uniformed man behind the big counter.

"I'm looking for Jerome Rasheed Cook," he said. "I'm his lawyer."

And, as before, the guard fiddled with his keyboard and brought the prisoner's name up on the screen.

"I'm sorry," he said, "something's wrong with the record. I don't think he's here."

"Where is he?"

The deputy looked troubled.

"It doesn't say. We had him here in June, but it doesn't show where he is now."

"What's he charged with?"

"I'm afraid I can't tell you that either. There's some problem here."

"How about a file, like a folder? Isn't there some other record but what's in that computer?"

"Yes, but my supervisor would have to get that for you. Only he's in training all week and won't be here."

Tubby shook his head. What else could he do? He left and reported back to the praline lady.

"That's just what I was afraid of," she said. "They done lost my boy."

"I'll see what I can do to find him," Tubby promised. More than anything else, he was curious. "What is your name, ma'am?"

"Pyrene," she said. "Miss Pyrene."

"If I find something out about Jerome, I'll let you know."

"Okay. I pray you do. God bless you."

"Thank you, ma'am. Bye-bye." Tubby walked off, eating his retainer.

CHAPTER

Twelve

TUBBY DROVE DOWNTOWN TO HIS OFFICE BUILDING. HE worked in the Place Palais on the forty-third floor. After navigating the spiral ramp of the vast parking garage and taking a series of elevators and making a couple of right turns he reached the door marked, in large but tasteful golden letters, DUBONNET & ASSOCIATES. It had once been TURNTIDE & DUBONNET, but Tubby's former partner seemed to have been swallowed up by the earth after getting too deeply involved in some of his clients' affairs.

Now Tubby worked alone, assisted by his secretary, Cherrylynn. The "Associates" in the title was just there in case he ever decided to hire some young lawyer to help him.

Tubby had only been to the office a couple of times in the week since he had returned from Florida. He was definitely resisting getting back into the swing of lawyering, and Cherrylynn had shown great dexterity in the art of getting continuances, postponing meetings, and generally handling his clients' business. She was getting to be so good he was thinking of calling her a paralegal and billing her time by the hour.

"Howdy, stranger," she greeted him when he walked in. Cherrylynn was about five-foot-two, 110 pounds, had brownish-blond hair, and she could look like a knockout when she dolled up. She cooked roasted peppers and shrimp, and had freckles that moved around when she grinned. When she saw Tubby the freckles moved.

"How's business?" he asked her, glumly grabbing a handful of accumulated phone messages.

"We've got more bills than we've got income, Mr. Dubonnet. It looks to me like it's time for you to get back to work."

"Thoughtful of you to share that with me, Cherrylynn. You may not realize it but I'm always working. Even when I sleep I'm dreaming about my clients."

"Some of them may be thinking you were a dream," she chirped.

"Okay. Let me get situated for a few minutes. Then bring me some files to look at. We'll go over the list and see what needs doing."

"I've already got everything organized for your review."

"I knew you would," he sighed. "Give me ten minutes or whenever you see I'm off the phone, then come on back and we'll spread stuff out."

"Right, boss."

His office was just behind the reception area. It was large and had a panoramic view of the city to the east—the French Quarter, the river's hairpin turn, and, in the far distance, the battlefield where Andy Jackson beat the bloody British in a town called New Orleans. One of Tubby's main relaxations was staring at the view he leased. Most striking to him were the weather patterns that developed before his eyes, mostly in the summer months. Frightening, massive, dark clouds would rise up over the Industrial Canal, like smoke billowing from a warehouse fire, except that these clouds dumped rain like Niagara Falls. With sun streaming in through his window, Tubby could watch these billowing thunderheads bear down upon Canal Street, scattering pedestrians like chickens, and then blot out all daylight and smash with a great rush of water into his building. His window glass would quiver and resonate like a drum. It was quite awesome and entertaining.

Tubby became aware that he was staring unproductively out

his window, still holding his batch of phone messages. He was back at work. Rats.

He sat in his familiar leather chair behind the handsome cypress desk that had come from the office of a now abandoned cotton compress in Avoyelles Parish. Idly he checked who had called him.

Jynx Margolis, whose divorce case would never end. Dr. Feingold, an old friend. Several calls from lawyers. A "Mr. Bubba Pender," whom he had never heard of, had called about a "potato patent," and Twink Beekman from Save Our River. On that slip Cherrylynn had written: "Wants you to meet him uptown to discuss lawsuit and suggests London Coffee House." That took kahunas. Ask your free lawyer to make house calls.

Cherrylynn buzzed to ask if he was ready, and he told her to come on in.

It took her about half an hour to bring him up to date on the status of everything currently going on in his office. She had also made him a list of things to do, organized by the priorities she had assigned to them.

"I want you to open a new file," he told her as they were finishing up. "Casino Mall Grandé, General Advice. Bills go to Jake LaBreau at the casino."

"What rate?" she asked.

"My top rate," he said with a broad satisfied smile. Even if he was bored with the law, he loved his top rate.

"This is your first casino client, boss."

"So?" He had the feeling she was going to try to ruin the moment.

"So nothing, I guess. I mean I just don't suppose I approve of it."

"Really? I didn't know you had an opinion about gambling, for or against." He was truly surprised. Cherrylynn had a rather checkered past. A wild youth, so to speak, with at least one loser ex-husband who came sniffing around every so often. There were lots of details Tubby didn't know, and didn't want to know. In the three years she had worked for him Cherrylynn had grown dramatically from sheepish, girlish receptionist to belligerent, irreplaceable, total manager. Still, for all her efficiency, she would mysteriously fail to report to work once or twice a year, and when she did show up after a day or two she was never on full power. Other than throwing a few sarcastic barbs her way, he didn't give her a hard time, even though these unexpected absences sometimes were quite inconvenient. Mental Health days, he figured. Sometimes he took those himself.

"Personally I think it's a massive rip-off, and all run by the Mafia," she said.

"Nobody forces people to go inside," Tubby said. "And in my opinion, heavier hitters than the mob are running casino gambling. It's a legitimate business now, and there aren't any tougher s.o.b.'s than legitimate businessmen. Anyway, all I'm doing is regular lawyer work—contract review, things like that."

"Well, it's not my place to say anything. I just have my opinion."

Tubby didn't reply.

"As long as I've started, I'll say one more thing, Mr. Dubonnet."

"Go ahead," Tubby said.

"I hope you won't hang out in that place too much. All that alcohol. It's an unhealthy atmosphere."

"Yeah, you're right." He was touched.

She gathered up her papers to go back to her desk.

"It's just that I worry about you, boss. Spending too much time around all that booze leads to nothing but trouble. I know that from experience."

"Yes, dear," Tubby said with a smile, and Cherrylynn left. He didn't dare tell her he was seriously considering buying Mike's Bar.

He could take care of one problem right away. Having a jailer say he could not locate Tubby's client and that it would be a week before the supervisor would look into the matter had given Tubby serious heartburn.

"Application for writ of habeas corpus," he scratched on a yellow pad. It had certainly been a while since he had filed one of these, but he thought he remembered the words.

> TO THE HONORABLE Michael J. Shistrunk, Judge of the Criminal District Court of the Parish of Orleans, State of Louisiana:
>
> The petition of Jerome Rasheed Cook, applying for writ of habeas corpus, with respect represents:
>
> 1. Jerome Rasheed Cook is presently in the custody of the Criminal Sheriff of Orleans Parish, Louisiana, and has been so detained for approximately six months.
>
> 2. Jerome Rasheed Cook is being held in custody without an order of Court. He was taken into custody by the New Orelans Police Department on or about the date aforesaid and thereafter placed in the custody of the Criminal Sheriff.
>
> 3. Petitioner was never charged with an offense by the State of Louisiana.
>
> 4. Petitioner has never been indicted upon any charge by the State of Louisiana.
>
> 5. No legal basis whatsoever has been shown for Petitioner's detention in custody.
>
> 6. The time limitations for instituting a prosecution against Petitioner have long passed.
>
> WHEREFORE, PETITIONER PRAYS THAT:

Tubby paused. His church background, sketchy though it may have been, always urged him to rebel at praying to the State of Louisiana. But what could you do? Just a form, right?

Petitioner prays, he continued, that:

> 1. A WRIT OF HABEAS CORPUS ISSUE HEREIN TO THE CRIMINAL SHERIFF OF THE PARISH OF ORLEANS, STATE OF LOUISIANA, to produce in open court, at such time and on a date to be fixed by this Honorable Court, the Petitioner herein, the person who is unlawfully confined, and then and there a true and correct return make of the reason and cause of the detention of Petitioner.
>
> 2. After due proceedings had, Petitioner be discharged and released from further detention and confinement, and all such orders issue which are necessary and proper in the premises and to which he may be entitled.

Tubby Dubonnet,
Attorney for Jerome
Rasheed Cook

He followed that up with an order for the judge to sign, and with that off his chest he felt immediately better.

In fact, that was a good note on which to end the day. He gave his draft to Cherrylynn and asked her to call his courier, Joe Boggs, to file the writ the next morning. He got his coat and, while she was not looking, slipped out the door.

CHAPTER
Thirteen

IT WAS NOT A LOUD NOISE, MORE A SORT OF A CLICK, but it was out of place. Tania's eyes snapped open. There it was again, a creak somewhere in the front room of her shotgun house. All of the lights were off. She had turned in early, as she had done each night since she had bumped off Charlie Van Dyne. And every night she had slept like a baby. There was a thump against a piece of furniture. Someone was in her house.

She jumped out of bed, trying to be silent but mostly intent on getting her nightrobe on because she had been sleeping without any clothes. She pulled the sash tight while creeping to the open bedroom doorway to listen. The nearest phone was in the kitchen, a few feet away down the hall, separated from the bedroom by a bathroom off to one side. She had known it was a mistake for a single woman in a big city not to have an extension near the bed, but she was so damn frugal. She had made one concession to city living, however, which was to keep a carving knife under her mattress.

When she heard the sound of a footstep in the kitchen she knelt down quietly beside the bed and slid out the knife, holding it tightly in one hand. With the other clutching her robe, she slipped to the doorway again.

There was another footstep.

"Yaah!" she screamed, a crazy sound. "Who's there?"

Shapes rushed at her through the darkness.

"Yaah!" she screamed hysterically. "Get out of here!"

Hands stretched through the doorway, tugging at her robe. The face that closed in on hers was the man of her nightmares, Hambone eyes, stupid and mean, crooked runny nose. She swept her knife upward. He tried to block her arm, and the sharp blade sliced over his fingers.

"Damn," he yelped in pain, and stepped back against the other dark figure rushing in behind him.

Her instinct was to throw the knife at them, cover her eyes with her hands, and run the other way. But there was no back way out. No escape but past these men.

"Yaah! Yaah!" Terrible noises that she didn't hear kept coming from her mouth as she marched into them, swinging and poking with her knife.

The man in front, the one she knew as Hambone in her mind, took the force of her attack. He grunted in surprise and anger when she pushed the knife hard and mad somewhere into his belly region, her fist reaching him and feeling his warmth. Now he was hollering too and was no longer blocking the hallway. The other man had retreated and pulled Hambone with him while she advanced. They backed into the recess where her kitchen sink was, and for a moment the way out was clear.

Tania ran past the men and toward the front of the house, through the dining room and living room. It took two hands to open the dead bolt on the front door so she threw down the knife in her haste and let her robe loose.

"Get the damn bitch," the wounded man commanded. He slumped against the refrigerator and groaned loudly when his partner let him go to run after Tania.

She was already out on the front stoop, then into the street running. Never had it seemed so quiet and empty. Parked cars lined both curbs but all the houses were dark and could just as well have been abandoned. She yelled at the top of her lungs and ran in the direction of Washington Avenue, her mind telling her to race toward her auntie's. No lights came on, but some dogs started barking. She heard her screen door bang shut and heavy running footsteps. This was her neighborhood, and she scampered around the corner thinking to lose him. But maybe it was his neighborhood, too. There was a good chance he could keep up and would hurt her auntie, too.

Now she was just running and scared—and feeling vulnerable as well with hardly any clothes on and air blowing around her legs. She heard him round the corner onto Annunciation Street and kick over a trash can in his way. She might be a little faster than he was, but she couldn't last long. There were no people in the street. No one was coming to rescue her.

TUBBY WAS DOING SOME LOW-KEY NEGOTIATING WITH Mr. Mike. The bar was open but might as well have been closed since no one had been in the place but the two of them, and Larry the ghost bartender, for the past forty-five minutes. This was a point not lost on Tubby, and though it helped him laugh off Mr. Mike's claims about the establishment's profitability, he secretly saw it as an advantage. Nothing wrong with a quiet place, he was thinking. Off the map, you might say. I could really get away from everything here.

They were doing some haggling about the hypothetical sales price, assuming Tubby wanted to own a bar, which he wasn't ready to concede. But truthfully the first number Mr. Mike had tossed out had seemed pretty fair. Still it might be a good idea to turn on the overhead lights at least long enough to see what all those shadows hid. He was trying to think of a tactful way to make that suggestion when the door buzzer sounded off twice in long grating blasts accompanied by insistent thumping. On the other side of the green glass panel was a woman's hysterical face.

"For Crissake, buzz her in, Larry," Mr. Mike said, "before she beats the door down."

Larry reached under the bar, and the door burst open. A small woman clutching a coat or a bathrobe around her rushed in. She stared blindly around her as the door clicked shut, taking with it all the street light.

"Well, little lady, you need some help?" Mr. Mike asked sweetly, making a halfhearted effort to raise himself from his chair.

Tubby was on his feet and approached the woman.

"Yes, I need help," she cried. She was shaking and wary.

"Sure," Tubby said, reaching her and offering his hand. "Are you hurt?" He was suddenly aware that she was almost naked.

"I think I'm all right," she said, trying to catch her breath. She took Tubby's hand, and let him lead her to a bar stool. "There's a man chasing me."

"Call the cops, Larry," Mr. Mike ordered. He was in motion now and made it across the floor to inspect the newcomer.

"No! Don't call the police," Tania cried.

The men all looked at her questioningly.

She looked back. "I don't want the police," she said quietly.

Mr. Mike and Larry could deal with that. It took Tubby another second, but he could deal with that, too.

Someone pounded on the front door, and the buzzer went off again.

"Take the girl upstairs, Larry," Mr. Mike said, and he pointed her to the back, hooking his index finger to show she was supposed to go behind the bar and through a passageway. She moved fast.

"You're the bartender," he told Tubby.

Tubby trotted behind the bar and pressed the door-release button. There was a loaded .45 next to the button and a police billy club with a leather wrist strap beside that. Tubby took the pistol and held it by his side.

A short heavyset man, dark complected, wearing a Saints warm-up jacket, stepped cautiously through the door.

"We're closed," Mr. Mike said.

"Young lady just come in here?" the man asked, trying to pick out landmarks in the soft glow of the Budweiser sign.

"Nobody here. Sorry, we're closed," Mr. Mike repeated.

The man took a step forward, and Tubby's thumb played with the safety on the .45.

"No drinks, bud. We're closed," he said.

The man studied the bar and the man behind it. He couldn't see anybody's hands. Then he made up his mind. He smiled broadly and stepped backward toward the door. He felt behind him for the handle.

"Yeah, well, I'll come back another time," he said, and pushed his way outside. The door swung shut, and the lock clicked.

"You're a natural as a bartender," Mr. Mike said. "You should see yourself."

Tubby exhaled and put the gun back on the shelf.

"Come on back down, Larry," Mr. Mike said, a little more loudly, and in a moment the bartender and Tania appeared from the blackness at the back of the room.

"Have a seat, girl." Mr. Mike indicated the seat next to his. "Bring the lady a drink, Mr. Dubonnet."

Tubby did, one for each of them.

"Young lady, you need some clothes on," Mr. Mike pointed out.

She smiled and clutched the robe tighter across her breasts. With her other hand she slammed back the shot of brandy Tubby had poured. He refilled her glass and asked, "Is there anything we ought to be doing?" He raised his eyebrows.

"I don't think so," she said.

"Do you live near here?" he asked.

"Yes, about three blocks away. This was the only place open."

"Well, when you get ready I can walk you home, or I can call you a cab."

She took another swallow and closed her eyes for a minute.

"No, I can't go home tonight."

"Then is there somebody we can call?" Tubby asked.

She paused again.

"No, there's nobody I want to call."

"Larry, go upstairs and see if you can't find one of Claudia's coats or something," Mr. Mike said.

"Well, where do you want to go?" Tubby asked her.

"Can I stay here?" Tania looked at each of them hopefully.

Mr. Mike reached into his shirt pocket to get his Chesterfields.

"You see a lighter by the register?" he asked Tubby. He drummed his fingers on the bar. "You can't really stay here," he told the woman. "I got to go home to my wife. These guys got to clear out, too. I mean, we're not set up for overnight accommodations." Tubby lit Mr. Mike's cigarette.

"You want to, you can come home with me," Tubby said.

She looked at him carefully, and he reciprocated, both of them looking for signs of dementia.

Neither one picked up any obvious indicators.

"I wouldn't want to put you out," she said politely.

"You gotta be kidding." Tubby slapped the bottle on the bar and laughed out loud.

"Hey, Tubby, was you gonna shoot that brother?" Mr. Mike asked.

"You've got a whole arsenal here," Tubby replied, nosing around under the bar.

"Very unfriendly to shoot the customers. Very bad for business. Lock it up, Larry, and let's get us into our cars."

Gallantly, Mr. Mike draped one of Claudia's old winter coats over Tania's shoulders. After checking his pockets and sticking a leather cash pouch under his belt, he made ready to leave. With

Larry watching their departure from the doorway, Mr. Mike got in his Oldsmobile and Tubby and Tania got into his Corvair.

"I live off Henry Clay," Tubby said.

"I know where that is," Tania said in a tired voice. It was near Persephonie, where Charlie Van Dyne used to live.

CHAPTER

Fourteen

TUBBY FLIPPED ON THE LIGHTS AND SHOWED TANIA THE
way into his house. He took her back to the kitchen and put her at
his little white table while he fixed a pot of coffee. He was a bit em-
barrassed about the dirty dishes lying around, but there was nothing much he could do. By that time they had each other's names.

"I imagine you're ready to get some rest," he said, counting out
scoops of Community Coffee.

"Yes, I'm very tired."

"I think I have some clothes upstairs that will fit you," he said.

She cocked an eyebrow at him.

"It's stuff that belongs to my daughters. Or belonged. They've
all grown up and have places of their own, or else live with their
mother, but they're always leaving things here. You can go through
them and pick out whatever you want."

"Thank you. This is all very nice of you." She had finished her
inspection of the room and relaxed. "I know I look very strange."

Like a hurricane refugee rousted in the middle of the night,
hair lopsided from sleep and without any clothes, he thought. He
also considered that her dark slender legs, demurely crossed but
bare to the thigh, were works of art, but he repressed that thought.

"Why don't you tell me why that man was chasing you?" he
asked.

"I think he wanted to kill me," she said simply.

"And why would he want to do that?"

"My younger brother got shot just a few weeks ago. I believe the guy who was after me was one of the same men who did it."

That got his attention.

"What's all this about?"

"Drugs." She spat the word out. "My brother was dealing their filthy drugs. Their crack and their chronic. They must have thought Kip took something of theirs. So they just killed him right out on the street and almost got my whole family killed. Maybe that was supposed to be a lesson for the other fools who work for them."

"And you?"

"And me what?"

"Are you involved with them in some way?" Tubby poured her a mug of coffee and set it in front of her.

She looked disgusted. "No, I don't have anything to do with anything sick like that." She held her cup in both hands and blew into it to make steam rise into her eyes.

"Tell me then, why are they trying to hurt you?"

"I don't know,"she sighed. "I'm very tired."

"Why don't you want to call the police?"

"Even if they did anything, they'd just make it more of a mess than it is. They wouldn't know where to start."

"I think you ought to call them. It's pretty obvious you're in danger."

"No," she said. "Look, can we talk about this in the morning?"

"Yeah, okay," Tubby said. "If you're ready I'll show you where you can stretch out."

He led her upstairs and showed her the guest bedroom. It was a lot neater than his. Lots of times one of his girls would sleep over here, and the closet was half full of abandoned apparel. He gave her some good towels, pointed out the bathroom, and said goodnight. He told her he would call her in the morning.

Tubby went into his own bedroom and checked the drawer in the little table by the bed to see if his own pistol was still there. It was, and he picked it up. It was an old and heavy gun, a Smith & Wesson .38. When you ordered shells for it at the gun store it was like ordering a double bourbon at a bar. People gave you respect because you were old. He checked to be sure that it was loaded and then went downstairs and made a tour of the house, looking carefully to be sure that all the windows and doors were locked.

He slipped out the back door and stopped to listen to the neighborhood sounds. A faraway train, a barking dog, and a faint siren were all he heard. The moon was up and very bright. He walked around the yard in a leisurely way, trying to look like maybe he was checking his flowers, keeping his gun down by his pants leg. He didn't want his neighbors to get excited. But nothing caught his eye except that the grass was wet with dew and glistened where moonbeams touched it.

He went back inside, checked the windows again, and climbed slowly up the stairs. He glimpsed Tania with a towel wrapped around her slipping from the bathroom to her bedroom. Sitting on his own bed he took off his shoes and loosened his belt. Without getting undressed he lay down on top of the covers and went to sleep.

He dreamed about tending bar at Mike's and having a gunfight with a stocky drug dealer whose name he never knew. The man was in a crouch, guns blazing from both hands. Tubby was fighting to get his safety off.

WHAT WOKE TUBBY THE NEXT MORNING WAS THE CLINK of dishes and the smell of bacon frying. For a second he imagined he was still married and that Mattie was fixing him breakfast. Then he remembered, she never fixed him breakfast.

He sat up and noticed that he had slept with his pistol beside him on the bedspread. Not too bright. It went back in its drawer. Tubby washed his face, changed clothes, and went downstairs.

Tania was wearing Debbie's jeans and Collette's LSU Tigers sweatshirt, and she was washing the dishes.

"Good morning," he said.

"Good morning," she replied cheerily. "I fixed some coffee and some bacon. Would you like some eggs?"

"Sure," he said, and sat down at the table. The clock on the stove glowed 6:32, and the sun was coming up outside. Tania brought him a cup of coffee and turned away to feed the toaster. She filled out the jeans a little too well, but he wouldn't complain.

"Sunny side up," he volunteered.

"Coming your way. Do you have to work this morning, Mr. Dubonnet?"

"Yes, after a while."

She cracked the eggs into the frying pan. "What do you do?" she asked.

"I'm a lawyer."

"Oh," she said.

"How about you?" Tubby asked.

"I work in a bank, but today I believe I'll call in sick."

"Good idea," Tubby said.

"What kind of law do you practice?"

"Civil, mainly. Some criminal. Whatever walks in the door. I like variety."

"Maybe you could help me."

"I'm already helping you," Tubby pointed out. "I gave you a place to stay, and I advised you to call the police."

"I need lawyer help." She set a plate of toast, bacon, and two perfect eggs in front of Tubby.

"Thank you." He smiled.

She smiled, too, but had a worried look in her eyes. She sat down and watched him eat for a minute.

"Do you believe in revenge?" she asked.

"Sure," Tubby said. "Somebody beats me in court, even if they deserve to, I get upset. And I hope some other case comes along so I can beat them."

"I mean real revenge, getting even." She lowered her head.

"That's a different business," Tubby said. "When I was a kid I might let the air out of somebody's tires, or something like that. In real life, though, if somebody messes me over, I don't necessarily do anything. I might just take that anger inside myself and put a stop to it. I might not want to keep spreading it around."

"I think sometimes you have to spread it around." She lifted her head and her eyes met Tubby's. Hers were very dark and deep like holes in the earth. The image disturbed him for some reason. "Sometimes if you keep the anger inside, you'll burst wide open."

"Hmmm."

She didn't continue.

"So, what did you do?" he asked her quietly.

"I'm not ready to tell you yet."

"Then I'm not ready to be your lawyer yet."

She took up his plate and carried it to the sink.

"Would it be okay if I stayed here today?"

"What do you do, at the bank where you work?" Tubby asked.

"I manage a branch in Gentilly. Look, you don't know who I am, but I am extremely honest. You can't imagine how funny I feel about asking you to let me stay here, but I can't go home right now, and I'm afraid of involving my family in this any more. . . . And, well, I'm just asking."

"I guess it would be okay," Tubby said. "Just don't do anything to bring any of those guys over here."

"I won't," she said. "And thank you very much. Most people wouldn't do this. And there're very few white men who would do this. You are a very nice man." She beamed at him and her eyes looked a little misty.

All Tubby could think about was how pretty her smile was and how her chest perked up the LSU Tiger. I ain't that nice a guy, he thought.

"How old are you?" he asked.

"Thirty-one," she said, looking him over.

Definitely in the right range, Tubby thought.

CHAPTER
Fifteen

THE RIDE UP TO TULANE UNIVERSITY BY STREETCAR took about half an hour. Tubby could just as easily have driven, but it was a very pretty morning. He had been standing on the corner when the car rolled to a noisy stop, and on impulse he had jumped aboard. There was a grand feel of luxury about the streetcar. Not only was it constructed of much better material, mahogany seats, stout leather straps, solid hunks of steel, than any form of public transportation put together in the past fifty years, and not only did you pass block after block of mansions oozing romance and old prosperity, but also the ride was slow as summer.

He was supposed to meet Twink Beekman for coffee at the Tulane student center to talk about whatever environmental lawsuit he might have in mind. Tubby had surrendered his place-to-meet argument without a fight. The streetcar ground to a halt in front of the campus, and he set off walking across the tree-lined quad.

It was familiar territory, his alma mater, but things kept changing. They had built a whole new law school, for example. It was about twice as big as the cramped old building where Tubby had learned his Palsgraf and Pennoyer, a shiny glass-and-brick monument to the endless profitability of training more and more attorneys. Inside the student center he was shocked to see that where once there was an Olympic-sized indoor swimming pool now there was the main campus bookstore. The basement underneath must have blue tiles on the walls and racing lanes painted on the floor.

Tubby had never met Twink Beekman, but the president of Save Our River accosted him as soon as he wandered into the cafeteria.

"Mr. Dubonnet," the tall, serious-looking young man said. He had on gold-rimmed glasses, a red lumberjack plaid shirt, and lots of curly brown hair.

Tubby said yes.

"I recognized you by your suit. You look like a lawyer."

"Too bad," Tubby said. He aimed to dress a little less well than his mint-condition colleagues, but by university standards he admitted he looked extra fine. They passed through the line for some swampy and very strong-looking coffee in a paper cup, then sat down at a table by the window with a view of a coed rugby match. A number of students said hi to Twink—some nodded respectfully at the man in the suit. When Tubby was a student they might have shot a straight guy like him the bird.

"Thanks for coming to talk to me, Mr. Dubonnet. Debbie says you're a great lawyer."

"My pleasure," said Tubby. "Tell me about your case."

"Actually, we've got several of them going on at once, but the law center is handling them, or else the Sierra Club Legal Defense Fund. They're really short-handed, though, and won't even talk to me right now about doing anything else."

Tubby nodded his head.

"We've had a project for the past year, involving making what we call a riverbank directory. The way it works is we map out all the companies and businesses along the riverfront. Right now we're trying to do all of Orleans Parish. We identify what each business is, like what it makes, and we try to identify what potential hazards it could pose to water quality."

"When you say water quality, you're talking about the Mississippi River?"

"That's right."

"That's pretty low quality to start with."

"Granted, but we're trying to get a handle on where the really dangerous stuff, like PCB's and heavy metals, might be getting into the water. And as we get better at it, and get a new crop of students next year, we want to expand the directory system into Jefferson Parish, then right on upriver to Baton Rouge."

"Very ambitious. How do you do your research?"

"Two ways, mainly. We do some basic mapping using readily available sources like the city directory and even the yellow pages, as well as some studies conducted by the Corps of Engineers, the EPA, and the Regional Planning Commission, and then we send out teams of volunteers to actually visit the businesses, or warehouses, on site, and see what's going on."

"And what's going on?"

"Well, as you might guess, every kind of trash you can think of is going into the river, as well as plenty of gas, diesel oil, and human waste. Most of the discharge we've detected is illegal, but it's relatively small stuff. Not likely to make a dent on the blue heron population of Plaquemines Parish, for example. A certain amount is just carelessness on the docks, or lax enforcement of the rules about bilge flushing, but now and again we run into things that make us perk up our ears."

"Like what?"

"For instance, just off the top of the list, there's an outfit called American Retro-Plastics that seems to be storing lots of rusty fifty-five-gallon drums on its property. Then there's Cargo Planners, which our student reporter says has stacks of wooden crates labeled 'batteries' sitting out in the weather. There's one called Bayou Disposal, which has a trucking depot maybe one or two hundred feet away from the actual water line. These guys collect hazardous waste, liquid by-products of oil refineries mostly, and truck it to an incinerator in northern Mississippi, where we think it's allowed to poison the atmosphere of most of mid-America.

They claim they just use the lot by the river as a maintenance shed, a place to repair their trucks and gas them up, nothing more, but we have information that they might be pumping stuff out of their trucks with hoses right into the river. There are other companies probably doing the same thing. These could be felonies, big time." Twink rapped his knuckles on the table in his excitement.

"Don't you turn complaints like that over to the Environmental Protection Agency or something?"

"Yes, but nothing seems to get done."

"So what's next?"

"Next is getting you to take the file, see what's involved, and bring a lawsuit against the offending companies and the EPA. The main objective is to force the EPA to devote resources to investigating the allegations we've made and see if a criminal prosecution can be supported."

"Correct me if I'm wrong," Tubby said, "but couldn't that take years?"

"Realistically, yes," Twink said sadly, "but you do what you can. Maybe we'll strike a nerve and get quicker results."

"Strike the government's nerve? You do that through politics and protest, not lawsuits," Tubby said. "And the press," he added, reluctantly remembering Kathy Jeansonne. "The government has lots of lawyers."

"But it is important, Mr. Dubonnet. If they really are pumping toxic waste straight into the river, it could, depending on what they are, do real damage to oyster harvests in the marshes or maybe even fishing in the Gulf."

"And kill some people?"

"Yes, if somebody was unlucky enough to drink the stuff or get immersed in it before it was diffused in the current."

"Okay," Tubby said. "I'll take a shot at it. Have you got a file for me to look at?"

"I sure do," Twink said, and he produced from the floor two accordion binders, each stretched big enough to contain an unabridged *Webster's*.

"Whew!"

"This isn't all of it, of course. We've got back-up studies that fill a whole file drawer, but this should get you started. And here's a list of ten companies we've had specific complaints about."

Tubby inspected the list and put it in his pocket. He accepted the rest of the baggage gracefully. He was doing this one for Debbie. Oh yeah, and the environment.

CHAPTER
Sixteen

TUBBY LUGGED THE FILES BACK TO HIS OFFICE AND told Cherrylynn to set aside a little time to organize them. As an afterthought he handed her Twink's list and asked her to begin getting what information she could about each of the companies, from American Retro-Plastics to Z-Train, Incorporated. He suggested that she call the secretary of state and see who ran each one.

He dumped the heavy files on the couch in his office, hung up his jacket, and called his home number. As expected, he got the answering machine. It told him he wasn't there to take his call but would call back as soon as possible.

"Hello, Tania," he said after the beep. "Pick it up, please. This is Tubby."

After a couple of seconds she came on.

"Hello?" she said.

"Hi. I'm just checking in to see how you're doing."

"I'm fine, thank you. I was just straightening up a little bit. I hope you don't mind."

"No, of course not." Please do. "Anything unusual around there?"

"Everything is fine. You've been so nice. Could I ask you for another favor?"

"What is it?" Tubby asked noncommittally.

"I suppose I have to go home sometime. I wonder if you would mind going with me."

"Just for company?"

"Just to see how everything looks. I'm very nervous about it."

"You probably should be nervous. Sure, I'll go with you. I've got a few things to clean up at the office, though."

"That will be just fine. I kind of feel like I'm on a vacation. I'm watching 'Oprah' and 'Donahue.'"

"Make yourself at home."

"Thank you," Tania said again, and they hung up.

Cherrylynn stuck her head in the doorway.

The secretary of state would only tell me about three companies at a time—some rule they have," she said.

"Come on in. What did you learn?"

"The first one on the list, American Retro-Plastics, is a Missouri corporation, and has a registered agent in Baton Rouge, George Guyoz."

"Okay," Tubby said. Guyoz was a lawyer he knew, and if need be he would call him and perhaps find out what the company did.

"The next two are Bayou Disposal and Cargo Planners," Cherrylynn continued. "And guess what."

"I give up."

"The incorporator of both of them is Bijan Botaswati, and he has an address on Burgundy Street in the French Quarter."

"Who are the directors?" Tubby asked.

"The only director listed is Bijan Botaswati. He's also listed as the president and secretary, and he's also the registered agent of both companies."

"Any other addresses?"

"Nope. Same address for everything."

Tubby wrote it down.

"Also a woman named Nicole called to confirm your fishing trip tomorrow." Cherrylynn's eyes positively gleamed with curiosity.

"Damn," Tubby said. "I'd forgotten about that. It's a sad case.

Poor old woman is terminally ill and wants to make plans for her artwork and cats."

"Fishing?"

"Strange, huh? But it's one of her only pleasures." Tubby shook his head at life's mysteries.

"Well, you might have a problem, boss. The judge signed your writ of habeas corpus for Jerome Rasheed Cook and set it for hearing tomorrow at nine o'clock."

Now what am I going to do about that? Tubby wondered. Fishing or the cause of justice?

Fortunately he was spared resolving the dilemma because the writ drew a quick response.

Hardly had the smirking Cherrylynn departed the room than she buzzed him to say that Captain Second Grade Passetta, director of Community Corrections, was on the phone.

"YEAH, MR. DUBONNET," HE BEGAN, "WE'VE DONE SOME research on our end here, on Jerome R. Cook, and looks like we don't have him."

"Where is he then?" Tubby demanded.

"He left our facility on June twenty-ninth in the custody of the sheriff of Pearl River County, Mississippi."

"Why was that?"

"They had a warrant for him for distribution of crack cocaine. I suppose the district attorney or sheriff here decided to let Mississippi have first shot at him."

"What was the charge against him in Orleans Parish?"

"That I'm not sure of. My records aren't complete on that. But the main thing is, he ain't in the custody of the New Orleans Sheriff's Department."

So Tubby got the Poplarville, Mississippi, sheriff's department on the phone. Not so much hassle there. Sheriff Bone came on the line right away.

"Cook?" he inquired loudly. "Yeah, we got Cook. What you want with him?"

"I'm trying to find out what he's been charged with. Is he serving time?"

"No, he's just biding time, eating county food. He hasn't been to trial yet. He's charged with selling dope."

"When is his trial date?"

"Now that I wouldn't know. I just hold 'em. And I've been holding him for a long time. Any more questions than that, you'll just have to take up with the district attorney."

ASSISTANT DISTRICT ATTORNEY SHERRY PEAVINE WAS DE-fensive.

"It does appear that a decision to prosecute should have been made before now. He has been in custody for an unusual amount of time, but there are very often reasons for that. He may have waived his right to a speedy trial."

"Do you see any waiver in his record?" Tubby asked.

"I don't really have a full record in front of me, Mr. Dubonnet."

"Has he been indicted?"

"Unfortunately, I can't seem to find either an indictment or a bill of information, but I've only been with this office since I got out of law school last May."

Tubby used his most magisterial voice.

"Miss Peavine, I'm going to send an associate of mine up to the Poplarville jail tomorrow morning. I expect you to instruct Sheriff Bone to release Mr. Cook forthwith to my associate or else I am prepared to sue your department for one zillion dollars for false imprisonment."

"Well, I don't know about that, Mr. Dubonnet."

"You'd better release him tomorrow or be prepared for one hell of a fight to keep him."

They both hung up in a huff. Tubby felt quite proud of himself. He called Raisin to see if he could drive up to Poplarville in the morning, and Raisin said he could.

TUBBY UNLOCKED HIS FRONT DOOR AND CALLED OUT, very loudly, "Tania, it's Tubby. I'm home."

"Okay." Her voice came from the back of the house.

He found her in the kitchen, sitting at the table with a cup of tea in front of her, looking happy to see him. She had tied a colorful purple-and-gold scarf she must have found upstairs around her hair, transforming herself into black princess housewife. The room was spotless. He complimented her.

"I wanted to do something to stay busy, and to show my appreciation."

"Very nice," he said.

"I've got all my things packed," she said with a laugh, pointing to her nightgown folded neatly on top of Mike's wife's coat. "I'll return the coat tomorrow."

Tubby smiled. "Are you ready to go?" he asked.

"Not really," she said. "I'm glad you're going with me."

"It's no problem," he said.

"We'll see when we get there," she said, and Tubby thought she was trembling a little.

"Just give me a minute." He went upstairs to get his handgun. He rummaged around for his holster but it had disappeared. He tried sticking the barrel of the pistol through his belt, first in front, then in back. No way. It must weigh ten pounds. I'm going to permanently damage myself with this, he thought. He put the gun back in the drawer and settled for his Uncle Henry pocketknife instead. Now what good would that do? It just made him feel better to have something in his pocket.

He got Tania into the car, and they drove toward the Irish Channel. He told her he had enjoyed her company and, truthfully, he was sorry to see her go. It was nice having somebody to come home to. She didn't say much. He picked up her scared vibes and turned on the radio, lucking upon Fats Domino. He hummed along to the music.

They had passed the National Maritime Union hall on Washington when she told him to turn off into a neighborhood of double shotguns with lots of gingerbread. She directed him onto Laurel Street and told him to pull over to the curb.

"This is my home," she said faintly, pointing to a narrow white single story. It was bracketed by nearly identical houses on either side, but Tania's was especially cozy-looking and had a well-tended flower garden and a sweet olive tree in its tiny front yard. He held open the iron gate for her, but she motioned him to go first.

She followed him up the steps and reached past him to test the door. It was locked, so she found the key under a potted cactus and opened the place up. Tubby went inside ahead of her. She reached around the doorsill and flipped on the lights. The room had been trashed.

Pictures were off the walls and broken, the couch was sliced up, its bright white stuffing haphazardly erupting, and books and magazines covered the floor.

Tania gasped and grabbed Tubby's arm. Her grip was almost painful. She pushed him forward, as her shield.

The dining room was more of the same. A glass cabinet was broken and what had been nice china was smashed and thrown around. Tubby was propelled into the kitchen, which was similarly ravaged. Tania looked carefully at the floor around the sink, but Tubby didn't see anything strange. He looked at Tania inquiringly, but she just shook her head in disbelief and pushed on until they were in the bedroom. Here also the mattress had been ripped open with a knife, no doubt, and clothing had been shredded and strewn about. Most of what could be damaged was.

She let his arm go and sank down on the bed, weeping. He sat down beside her to offer some comfort, but she got up right away and began digging out torn photographs from the pile on the floor. She was sobbing in great gulps. She wandered into the kitchen crying, picking up broken things and shaking her fists. Tubby just sat on the bed and listened to her going through the wreckage of her house. It had been a thorough job—a nasty job. The TV was on the floor broken. Destruction, not stealing, was the message.

The crying had stopped so he got up and went to the front of the house. Tania was standing by the front door, looking outside. He went up and stood silently beside her.

"The world's burdens are heavy," she said.

Tubby couldn't think of anything to add to that.

"Would you like me to help you clean up?" he asked.

"Not now. I need to face this on a new day." She started shivering. "I'm frightened to be here," she said.

Tubby put his arm around her shoulder and they stood like that for a little while, watching the street get dark.

He felt her reluctance to bring it up.

"Do you want to come back to my place?" he asked.

"That would be awfully nice," she said, exhausted.

AFTER SHE GATHERED UP SOME CLOTHES FROM THE heaps on the floor and found her toothbrush, they locked the house up and drove back to Tubby's. He ordered pizza from Café Roma, and when it came they ate in front of the TV, watching "Matlock."

"Do you want to tell me more about how all this involves you?" he asked her once during a commercial.

She looked like she was about to, but then she just shook her head. They didn't do too much other talking. It was comfortable though, kind of like old friends.

After the news they said goodnight, and Tania went upstairs to bed. Tubby went around the house checking his perimeter again, then went upstairs himself. This time he got undressed and crawled between the sheets. He was drifting off when he heard Tania moving around. He heard her leave the guest bedroom and walk softly down the hall. She hesitated outside Tubby's door, then came in. She sat lightly on the bed.

"What is it?" he whispered.

"I just felt very lonesome, and I wanted to be with you."

"Oh," Tubby said, but he didn't tell her to leave.

"I don't know what it's like to trust a white man," she said.

He sat up and put a pillow over his lap.

"That's not so surprising," he said.

"I was raised to treat everybody alike, but even when white people seem real friendly, I'm always waiting for the other shoe to drop."

"For their real selves to come out?"

"Yes."

"It's complicated," he said.

She took his hands in hers.

He had never been in a bed with a black woman before, even though you couldn't really say they were in bed together. He smelled the shampoo in her hair and felt the warm pressure of her thigh against his knees. He was helplessly aroused.

She bent down and kissed him on the cheek and whispered, "You're a nice man."

There was that misconception again.

Then she stood up and pulled her nightgown straight. She waved and whispered, "Good night." And left.

Tubby sank back into the covers.

What the hell was that? he asked himself. A tease? But he

didn't think so. He wanted to believe she was the real thing. He thought about tiptoeing over to the guest bedroom and continuing the conversation, but he found he was struggling, too. Safety for the single always lies in inaction. He could try to get a grip on this in the light of day. He fell asleep.

IN HIS DREAM, TANIA LAY DOWN BESIDE HIM AND lightly touched his hair with her fingers. He stroked her back tentatively, and stared into deep eyes close to his own, asking questions. Her answer was to pull his mouth to hers. While they kissed, their hands began a gentle exploration of each other's body under their nightclothes. He felt her soft breasts, nipples erect, and thought how smooth and warm she felt everywhere. He wished he hadn't eaten three-fourths of a large pizza. She ran a hand down his back and on down to his hips. Suddenly Tubby was ravenous again. He rolled her on top of him and began seeking sweet places to feast. The moon's glow from the window lit her neck and she moved with him.

Something he had read in the bar journal about having sex with clients flashed through his mind.

"I'm not your lawyer, of course," he whispered hoarsely.

"No, no," she moaned. "You're whatever you want to be to me, baby."

She rose, hands pressed on his shoulders, and slid herself up and down on him. Nothing but panting and rich feelings now. The bed creaked mightily.

CHAPTER

Seventeen

TUBBY WOKE HIMSELF UP SHORTLY AFTER FOUR O'CLOCK.
He was alone.

"Goodness," he muttered to himself.

A great deal of the motivation for taking Nicole Normande
fishing had not-so-mysteriously vanished, but when a lady has
agreed to be dressed and ready by five in the morning, only a real
jerk calls in sick. Tubby also felt that escaping a morning-after
scene with Tania was a good idea, though he couldn't have explained why since all the best parts had been in his fertile brain.

He got up quietly, showered, and left a short note for her. He
signed it "Nice Guy." Dressed in funky khaki pants and a sweatshirt, he checked the boat for life jackets. Once he had hidden a
bag of money in that same spot. He saw that his ice chest was relatively mold-free, and loaded up two full gas tanks. It didn't take
long to hitch the trailer to the car, even though it was pitch black.
Tubby was an old hand at quick flights from the city.

By 5:15 he was double-parked in front of the Royal Street address Nicole had given him. When he tapped on her door she appeared, freshly scrubbed and very appealing in blue jeans and a
couple of shirts. She didn't ask him to hang around while she got
her makeup on. She was ready.

In no time they were cruising through Chalmette on Judge
Perez Highway, drinking coffee from the thermos Nicole had
brought. Tubby's mood had shifted dramatically, and he was now
thinking what a great idea this excursion was. They passed the last

traffic light at Paris Road, and presently the homes and schools gave way to farms and then cypress swamp.

Not much farther and they turned onto a smaller road and soon crossed over a narrow, wooden-railed drawbridge where they saw their first shrimp boats bobbing picturesquely at their moorings. Their way ran straight along the bayou with house trailers and rickety fishing camps to the left and tin boathouses and docks jutting into the water to the right. After a few minutes Tubby pulled up next to one of the camps, which he said belonged to an old man he knew named Nolan. Nicole got out and watched while he checked the fishing tackle again and unplugged the trailer lights. Then she yelled directions as he backed across the road and eased the boat down a rough concrete ramp into the bayou. She held the rope to keep their humble vessel from floating away while Tubby parked the car next to Nolan's camp.

The sun was just coming up when the motor obliged them by catching, and they puttered out over the water. White egrets and blue herons flew easily across the stream ahead, announcing their approach. The bayou was calm and flat, but for ripples here and there that showed the tide was pulling them out. A fish broke the surface in front of them, a promising sign.

Without talking much, Tubby and Nicole watched the fishing camps give way to marsh grass and wider and wider vistas. Soon there was nothing but clear blue sky and a broad channel of shining blue water, and grasses all shades of green running to the horizon. The white birds multiplied and sailed away on business of their own.

Their bayou emptied into a lake so wide that it could have been mistaken for open gulf. Tubby guided the boat to a point along the marsh shore and then cut the motor and pitched over the anchor. Two oil rigs were visible in the far distance, and scattered here and there were outposts of trees, little dots in a big saltwater lake. A morning breeze rocked the boat and tossed up sprinkles of cold salty water. Except for the waves slapping the wood and an occasional bird cry, the only sounds were ones Tubby and Nicole made.

"Let's see what we got here," Tubby said, getting out his tackle box and putting it between his feet. "The trout like cockahoes the best, but we'll have to try a lure on them today." Skillfully, he tied leader and lure on one of the lines and handed the rod to Nicole. While he repeated the process on his own rod, he watched her try to cast. The first time she got it out about a yard before the line stopped and the hook swung malevolently back at the boat. The second time she sailed a beauty out about fifty feet and dropped it near the grass just right.

"You've done this before," Tubby commented dryly.

"I grew up fishing," she said. "My mother and I used to go out on the lake all the time where we lived in Tennessee. We fished for bass."

Finally I meet a woman who grew up fishing, and there's a lady at home who believes I'm a nice guy, Tubby thought.

"What about your dad?" he asked.

She brushed a strand of hair out of her eyes. "He wasn't around much," she said.

Tubby watched his pole. "If we're lucky," he said after a while, "we'll hit a school of sacalait when they're hungry. We might bring in thirty or forty fish in a matter of minutes."

"Do you need a license for this?"

"Uh, yeah," Tubby said. "I didn't think to ask if you had one."

"I don't. Should I be worried?"

"Not you," Tubby said. It would be his boat that would get impounded.

"What's the name of this . . . ," she gestured at the water.

"I think it's part of Lake Petit. I'm not real sure anymore. See those trees out there?" He pointed at a stand of dying cypress poking from the water half a mile away.

"When I first started fishing out here, that used to be an island. It's still on the charts as an island. I've walked on it—even hunted rabbits on it. In fact, there used to be several islands out here. Now we're just about in the Gulf of Mexico."

"What happened?"

"Erosion. Salt water from the Gulf coming into the marsh from all the canals the oil companies dredged killed the grass. The wake of ships in the ship channel and the Gulf Outlet washed away the soil. You hear lotsa theories. I can tell you a bunch of land has disappeared in a short time."

"Unreal," she said.

The morning progressed peacefully, that is, without too many fish. Tubby learned that Nicole was from around Memphis, that she had a brother who had done well for himself but who, she said vaguely, lived in a different world, that she had come to New Orleans to work for a tomato-packing company, and that the casino was a big step forward.

They pulled in lots of hardhead catfish—the kind that stab you, and you can either throw them back to catch a second time, keep them for crawfish bait, or shoot them, whichever seems like the least trouble. Crawfish rejoice over dead hardheads or just about any kind of rotting fish or meat.

Their biggest excitement was a strike on Nicole's line that bent her rod, went around and under the boat, and had them both shouting advice to each other. She finally reeled it close enough to the surface for Tubby to recognize her catch as a stingray with three-foot wings. Then the game became trying to save the tackle. Eventually Nicole got the frightening creature to the side of the boat, and Tubby reached gingerly into what may have been its mouth with a pair of pliers and twisted out the hook. It slid into the water and with a flip was gone. But of trout or crappie, not a one.

A wind picked up while their battle with the stingray was raging, and the boat began to bounce around in an unhealthy way. Little whitecaps came rolling across the lake.

"Maybe we better go back in," Tubby said. Nicole was hanging on with both hands.

The ride back up the bayou was rocky but they enjoyed flying with the wind behind them. Even though the sun stayed bright, they were both cold, shaken up, and wet by the time they made it back to the boat launch.

"Great fun," Nicole said, as she clambered out of the boat, shivering.

"Yeah, but I kinda wish we'd caught a fish," Tubby said grumpily.

They stopped off at a restaurant named Ivanho's on the way back, and had a hearty meal of grilled redfish and pompano from the kitchen. The hush puppies were the fluffiest he had ever had. Tubby told her a little about the Save Our River case. She seemed to be interested in a lot of the same things he was. A couple of beers apiece, and they were both feeling cheerfully tired by the time Tubby navigated back to Royal Street and Nicole's front door.

"Would you like to come up and see the place?" she asked.

The opportunity of a lifetime, but Tubby's brain was hopelessly confused. Two superlative women at once was an awful lot to grasp.

Nicole laid her hand on his. "I had a wonderful time. Would you like to come in for a beer?"

"I've really got to go," Tubby said gruffly. "I have to get the boat put away. I had a good time, too. I'll call you. We'll do it again."

"Okay." She withdrew her hand, collected her purse, and got out of the car.

"Bye," she said succinctly, and ran up the steps to her building. Tubby watched her unlock the door and disappear inside.

"Bye," he said.

• • •

TUBBY GOT THE BOAT BACK HOME AND UNHITCHED. HE
stowed the gear, and then he went to the house.

"Tania," he called when he opened the door. "It's Tubby." No
answer.

On the kitchen table there was a note.

> Dear Tubby,
>   Thank you for everything. You were a big help.
>
>   Tania

Deflated, Tubby walked distractedly around the downstairs of
his home. He sat at the kitchen table and thought. Then he gave it
up and phoned Cherrylynn for his messages. She reported that
Raisin was on his way in from Mississippi.

CHAPTER
Eighteen

RAISIN DELIVERED JEROME RASHEED COOK UP TO THE forty-third floor. Cherrylynn announced them, victory making the pitch of her voice rise to a new high, and Raisin rolled Jerome through the door like a new car he'd just won on a quiz show.

Jerome was a short fellow, dressed in oversized blue jeans and a T-shirt, probably the same clothes he'd been arrested in more than six months before. He looked around the room slowly and uncertainly, dazed by the sudden transition into freedom.

Tubby came around the desk to shake his hand. Jerome's grip was a little weak, but his eyes said he was ready to be happy.

"Sit down, man," Tubby offered. "Let's hear your story."

Cherrylynn brought coffee.

Jerome didn't mind talking. He had been waiting a long time.

"I sold some stuff," he said. "It was only the one time. Really. But it was bad, and the people I sold it to turned me in. It wasn't my fault it was bad. The man I got it from set me up. He's the one that ought to pay."

He had told that to a sheriff's investigator at the Orleans Parish jail. He had named the man he bought drugs from. The investigator suggested maybe they would just let Jerome go, but Jerome said that, when they did, he was going after his supplier. That had been a mistake. Next, he was handcuffed in the backseat of a police car headed out of town. They had been met by a Mississippi sheriff at the Pearl River turnaround, and he was transferred to the sheriff's car. For the past six months he had been sitting around in the Poplarville jail.

"Who was your supplier?" Tubby asked.

"A guy they called Charlie Van Dyne," Jerome said, "and he deserves whatever he gets."

"I never heard of him," Tubby said.

"I ain't going to bother about him," Jerome said. "If he leaves me alone, I'll leave him alone. How'd you find me?"

Tubby told him about the praline lady's vigil outside the jail at Tulane and Broad, and Jerome covered his face with his hands and cried like a baby.

"She's the sweetest lady," he finally said. "She loved me all my life."

"Go see her right now and promise her you won't sell drugs anymore."

"I sure will," Jerome said. "I'll never forget her, or you."

"After you say your hellos, I want you to come back and see me, Jerome. You've got a lawsuit against the sheriff I want to talk to you about."

"Yes, sir. What do I owe you now?"

"That's what the lawsuit is for."

RAISIN SAID HE WOULD RUN JEROME UP TO TULANE and Broad.

"I don't guess he remembers how to ride the bus," he said, to explain his kindness.

CHAPTER

Nineteen

ON SATURDAY MORNING TUBBY WENT SHOPPING IN THE French Market for a few of the things he liked to buy there: some nice big garlic, loaves of fresh seeded bread, a can of virgin olive oil, and some red peppers from the Progress Grocery. The market smelled like New Orleans should, a mixture concocted of crates of garden produce, coffee brewing, beignets coming out of the cooker, and the river rolling on just a few arpents away.

He felt "bright-eyed and bushy-tailed," as his father used to say, and he realized that he had Jerome Rasheed Cook to thank for that. It was just amazing what a win could do. He was interested in being a lawyer again.

The enthusiasm was so strong that Tubby thought he might check in on the mysterious Bijan Botaswati, incorporator of Bayou Disposal and Cargo Planners, as long as he was already in the Quarter and legally parked.

The address on Burgundy was a bar called The Hard Rider. The neighborhood here was mostly residential, a lot of gays, a lot of medical students, a lot of time-shares, and a lot of shuttered court-yards that told you nothing, just as intended. The bar was open, but not hopping. Tubby made out two fellas yining and yanging at the dark end. There were a couple of Foosball tables in the center and some hanging ferns for decor. It smelled like smoke.

Tubby took one of the tall chairs and ordered a Dixie beer, just to be sociable. The bartender was a small Vietnamese woman wearing black pants with suspenders over a frilly white shirt.

"No Dixie," she said, mopping up in front of him with a towel.

"Make it a Bud then." The whole world served your basic Bud. She brought him a bottle and a glass.

"Two dollars," she said, and he handed her a five.

When she came back with the change he asked, "Is Mr. Botaswati here?"

"Not here. Three, four, five." She counted out his change.

"Can you tell me where I might find him?"

"Not here. He's got many businesses."

"Do you think he might be in today?"

"Sometime he comes by," she said with a shrug. "Sometime no."

"It's very important that I talk to him. If he is the same Bijan Botaswati I think he is, there are some people in Pakistan who want to do business with him. There could be a lot of money in it. Will you tell him?"

"Yeah, sure. If I see him I tell him."

"Here's my card." Tubby took one from his wallet and wrote on the back, *Important proposition.*

"Tell him he must call me soon."

"Okay," she said, taking the card and moving away toward her two other customers.

Tubby drank his beer and looked around the place. New Orleans prints on the wall. Wineglasses hanging from the ceiling on a wooden rack. How would this atmosphere work in Mike's Bar? He flinched. The old-timers would curse and shun him. He left the three dollars on the bar in hopes that she would remember to deliver his card and walked out.

Tubby recalled that he had not had any lunch. A beer in the middle of the day was not routine for him, and it put him in a mind to stroll around the Quarter and forget life's troubles. Surely there would be no harm in detouring up Bourbon Street to take in the sights.

He walked around the corner on St. Ann, sidestepping a curvaceous woman wearing hot pants who cast him an alluring eye. Was she nothing but misfortune and trouble, or was she a lonesome tourist from Germany, anxious to find Pat O'Brien's? Always hard to tell.

He passed her by with a polite smile. In the curbside litter he saw the sparkle of a strand of beads. In New Orleans you see beads on the street all the time, and you don't know until you stop and pick them up whether they're extremely valuable, like pearls a movie star might have dropped, or funky Mardi Gras beads from Taiwan. Tubby bent over. These were sort of neat, a string of multicolored glass and clay. There was something he liked about them, so he absently slipped them into his pocket and walked on. He was just about to Bourbon Street when he heard a familiar voice calling his name.

Tubby turned around and saw Nicole Normande, wearing a red dress tied at the waist that made his eyes pop out.

"Hello, fishing buddy," she said. "What brings you out to the French Quarter?" She looked bright and sunny.

"I was just thinking about lunch. And you?"

"Running an errand for Jake. Meeting with a nonprofit group that asked us for a contribution. And thinking about lunch."

"Well, why don't you join me?"

"I'd love to." She smiled.

"How about Mr. B's?"

"That sounds just perfect."

"Then here we go." Tubby offered an arm and she took it firmly. Together they strolled among the frolickers of Bourbon Street, chatting like old chums.

"I'M RARELY DISAPPOINTED HERE," TUBBY REMARKED contentedly, watching the waiter place a china plate of shrimp stuffed with crabmeat in front of him and a cool fried-chicken salad in front of Nicole. He spread the last of his baked Brie on a bit of French bread and popped it into his mouth. He motioned for the waiter to take the empty plate away.

"I think it's so cute the way they make carrots curl up," she said, pointing with her fork.

He was distracted by the cherry tomato she slid past her perfect lips.

"Do you come here often?"

"As often as I can," Tubby recovered. "Thank you," he said to the waiter, who poured the water and sank the slice of lemon in his glass.

"Mine is delicious. Would you like a taste?"

"Sure."

She filled her fork carefully and then extended her arm quickly across the table and fed him.

It was a most pleasant experience, the personal delivery more than the tasty food.

"Very good," he sighed.

"Have some more."

"No." He couldn't.

"It's almost a shame to use up your appetite," he said. "They serve great desserts."

"Don't worry about me," she said.

And she was true to her word. When the tiny remains of his fish had been cleared away, she happily ordered a white chocolate brownie covered with fudge and ice cream, and Tubby, challenged, called for bananas Foster shortcake. She ate hers all up and sat back, coffee cup in hand, looking like she could do it again. Tubby was blissed out on sweetness.

"Now what?" he asked.

"I suppose I should show my face at the casino," she said. "Would you like to keep me company?"

"I really ought to go home and mow the grass, or something. There are things I need to do." But he couldn't actually think of any.

"Oh, come on. Think of it as work if you want to. Legal research. You need to get to know your client better."

He smiled at her, thinking it over.

"You can even bill your time. This should be a money-making relationship for you."

That did it. "I'd be delighted." He beamed.

Tubby paid the check, and they went out the revolving doors onto Royal Street, where patrons of costly antique shops dressed in tweeds with elbow patches mixed with teenagers wearing ripped blue jeans and silver rings in their noses.

It was just a few blocks walk to the casino. There were some fears, before the first one opened, that round-the-clock gambling would absorb all the tourist dollars that were the life's blood of the Vieux Carré, and still the reviews were mixed. Some of the club owners complained. Others were happy. The French Quarter had survived war, epidemic, and fire. It had hidden queer joints, quadroon balls, and whorehouses aplenty. It ought to be able to handle a few li'l ol' casinos.

They enjoyed the walk, and Tubby was even telling jokes by the time they entered the lavish halls of Casino Mall Grandé. The white-suited attendants, the plainclothesmen, even the waitresses acknowledged Nicole when she came in—the pretty boss in the red dress.

"Where should I begin my research?" he asked.

"I'll show you," she said, and led him through a maze of tables to one on a platform where they were playing blackjack. There was an empty seat, in contrast to most of the tables, where people watched and waited for a chance to sit down and wager. "Here's where you start," she said.

Tubby sat. He noticed the gold sign by the dealer that said the minimum bet was $100 and the limit was $5,000. This could be why there was an available chair.

"Uh, Nicole," he began.

"Hush," she said, rubbing him on the shoulder. She reached over him and placed a stack of black chips by his fingertips.

"Now let's see what a lucky man you are," she whispered in his ear.

She stood behind him, occasionally pressed against his back, and even through the fabric of his suit he got a sensation that was extremely exciting.

Tubby blackjacked on his first hand.

"Oh, goody," he said.

"You're starting out hot," Nicole laughed.

He doubled up on the next hand and won again. A waitress placed a cocktail by his elbow and miraculously he discovered that he was thirsty for it.

He doubled up and won. His adrenaline rushed. Nicole was giggling and squeezing his shoulder. The other players were nodding in appreciation and envy.

Time flashed by and his stack grew into a pile. He didn't win every hand, but he was marvelously lucky. When he passed $30,000 he started betting the limit on each hand and doubling up at every opportunity. Nicole stayed at his back and got him whatever he wanted from the bar. He tipped the waitress with $20 chips and she stayed very close by. He was afraid to pause, or even go to the bathroom, for fear of ending the streak.

Tubby counted $88,000 and sat back.

"That was my grandfather's age when he died. I've got to stretch my legs." He was both exhausted and exhilarated. "Get me out of here," he begged.

He shook hands all around, tossed a little handful to the dealer, who announced, "Taking tip," and let Nicole help him carry his basket of chips to the window to cash in. He took a thousand in bills and the rest in a check.

"Fresh air," he demanded, draining the last of something alcoholic from the plastic glass he found in his fist.

He was in the backseat of a taxi, jabbering about what a rush it had been, rolling his head from side to side to let the night breeze blowing in through the cab window cool him down.

Then Nicole was paying the driver and showing him into the door of her quaint and expensive Creole cottage. While he sat on a stool she mixed them each a drink and turned on some music. He raved about her beautiful paintings and choice of cookbooks.

Then they were necking while dancing in the living room. His hands roamed over her shoulder blades while she played with his sandy blond hair.

CHAPTER

Twenty

ON SUNDAY MORNING, TUBBY TOOK A WALK IN AUDUBON Park by himself and tried to figure out what he felt about Nicole. He gave it up. On Sunday afternoon, he went to pick up Collette. At one time, he would have asked his daughter to meet him somewhere, the object being to avoid a run-in with the child's dear mother. But for the time being, at least, things were all hunky-dory between Tubby and Mattie. He was current on his child support and had even come up with the bucks to send their middle child, Christine, on a three-week trek to Europe with her Newman class. Her tuition was up to date, as was Debbie's tuition at Sophie Newcomb. This had never happened before, and might never again.

Anyhow, Mattie was sure to greet him at the door with a smile when he showed up today. He liked her much better this way. The old flame still flickered sometimes, whether he wanted it to or not, but it wore him out like nothing else to fight with her.

He rang the bell, always a strange experience at a house he had called home during the seventeen years of their marriage. It was still hard not to feel a little pang of guilt when he saw that the bushes needed a trim. All the shrubs missed his attention. Jesus, she was even letting the azaleas die.

"Hi, toots," Mattie said from the doorway. "Checking on the flowers?" She was casually dressed in shorts and a green blouse that set off her bright red hair, and she seemed to be slightly giddy with drink.

"Come on in," she said. "Collette is on the phone."

in a war fought over South American ruins, who learned to love and, yes, respect the gorgeous, nubile blonde who led him into battle.

On account of the company he was with, Tubby was going to enjoy it more than he would ever care to admit.

CHAPTER

Twenty-One

ON MONDAY MORNING, TUBBY BEGAN DICTATING AN AF-
fidavit of death, domicile, and heirship and a petition to probate
the testament of Potter Segnac Aucoin. He knew the legal words
by heart; they came automatically from the formulary implanted in
his mind by years of practice. He just had to insert the names, and
that was the tough part.

He sketched out a descriptive list of assets and liabilities, using
the documents Edith had dropped off. The list was short and un-
complicated enough that the succession could probably be opened
and closed, all debts paid and all property delivered to Edith in a
matter of days. Very tidy, Potter's life. He had made a lot of money
as a free-wheeling businessman in the realm of international welfare, and his bank accounts were easily identified and well stuffed.
Tubby could be handsomely paid just for getting it all in order—
pulling down the final curtain on the life of the late Mr. Aucoin.
There were just a few nagging problems.

He called police headquarters and asked for Detective
Kronke. He was a little surprised when he got through to him.

"Good morning, Detective, this is Tubby Dubonnet."

"How are you today, Mr. Dubonnet? What can I do for you?"

"I wondered if you were making any progress on the Aucoin
murder case."

"We're still actively pursuing some things. Where are you?"

"Me? At the office."

"I would like to talk to you. Would it be convenient for me to come over now?"

"This minute?"

"If it wouldn't be inconvenient."

"No, sure. Forty-third floor."

"I know. We'll be there shortly."

Tubby hung up. It was definitely intimidating having a police detective anxious to talk to you, however polite he was. Tubby asked Cherrylynn to hide anything incriminating while he cleaned off his desktop and generally fidgeted until Kronke arrived.

CHERRYLYNN MADE THE POLICEMAN COMFORTABLE IN one of the client chairs facing Tubby. Fortunately there was no "we"; Kronke was alone. He was shorter and rounder than Tubby, but Kronke had some muscle mass packed inside his gray blazer. He was clean-shaven and bald and held a guileless, friendly expression on his smooth face.

"Quite a view you have, Mr. Dubonnet."

"It's pretty spectacular," Tubby agreed.

"So, I'm looking at the French Quarter. And there are the projects. Boy, from up here they look just the same."

The distant wail of a siren, blown up by the wind, reminded Kronke of his mission.

"You're handling Aucoin's estate, right?" he asked Tubby.

Tubby admitted he was.

"Have you noticed anything out of the ordinary? Any unexplained transactions?"

"No. It's all quite ordinary."

Tubby wasn't about to tell him about Kathy Jeansonne's call.

"Do you know much about Mr. Aucoin's export business?" Kronke asked.

"Only what I can tell from the books. The CPA has looked at them, too. We see money going in, money coming out. Nothing irregular. But actually how the business worked? I have only the vaguest notion. There's a filing cabinet full of invoices and correspondence at the shop. You're welcome to look through it. Broussard, the foreman, might know something, but I doubt he knows a lot, other than the day-to-day mechanics of shipping."

"Did Aucoin have any partners, any business associates?"

"None at all."

"Oh, well," Kronke sighed. He shrugged to say he'd tried.

"What are you looking for, Detective?"

"A place to start," Kronke said. "We don't really have a lead right now. The man had no enemies anyone knows about. He worked alone. I would call his death accidental—maybe a bad fall—except there were signs of a struggle in his shop, and, of course, somebody had to slide the hatch cover shut on the barge."

"No prints on anything?"

"Footprints, drops of blood, some other interesting things, but on a wharf where men work all day . . . ?" He spread his hands to show what a problem it was.

"It's a complete mystery to me, too," Tubby said.

"Did you ever know Mr. Aucoin to take drugs?"

Ahh. Tubby had already thought about his answer to this question, and he had decided that what he knew about Potter's secrets and personal failures was going to remain between Tubby and the dead.

"I never saw him take any, if that's your question, but in his younger days he may well have."

"Just casually, or on a regular basis?"

"I don't know," Tubby said. "I'm sure it was a long time ago, though."

"So you wouldn't think he bought or sold any kind of, uh, drugs or anything. He was, you know, in the export business."

"I certainly would not think so. Why the questions?"

"I guess it won't hurt to tell you. One of the things we found when we looked through his office, in that filing cabinet you were talking about, was a quantity of cocaine."

"How much of a quantity?"

"About half a kilogram. That's enough to last your social user a lifetime. What do you think?"

"I don't know what to think. It doesn't fit the picture I have of Potter."

"Yeah, but there it is."

There it was. Detective Kronke poked and shoved it around for another ten minutes, but it didn't go away.

"You used to be partnered up with Reggie Turntide, didn't you?" he asked as he got up to leave.

"That's right," Tubby said warily.

"He disappeared, didn't he? Did they ever find him?"

"No."

"That was strange, wasn't it?"

Tubby just nodded.

After Kronke left, Tubby closed his eyes and tried to relax. That didn't work so he called Kathy Jeansonne at the paper. He talked it over again with her, but she did not tell who her source was, and she did not tell him anything else about the police investigation. Tubby got the impression she had more interesting things on her mind—that the news value of the man in the vat of oil was fading fast.

As an afterthought he also asked her if she had ever heard of Bayou Disposal or Cargo Planners. No, she hadn't. Gotta go.

NOBODY OWNS THE LAND BETWEEN THE LEVEE AND the river. It is the property of all of the people. That's the Napoleonic Code. You lease it from the people, represented by the

Port Authority or the Levee Board. That's the Municipal Code. Tubby got Cherrylynn to walk over to the Levee Board to see if she could get copies of the leases of each of the companies on Twink Beekman's "bad guy" list. See what information you can pick up, he told her. And after that, if she got a chance, he asked her to review the Save Our River file to see what specific complaints had been made about the various shippers, grain elevators, warehouses, and manufacturers plying their rough and noisy trades there. It would be a challenge for her, he said, like a college research project.

"Sure, no problem," she said.

Tubby was just checking. Cherrylynn's résumé showed a degree from Walla Walla College, and he suspected she had just made it up. But Cherrylynn hadn't even blinked.

He told her he would be back later. It seemed Mr. Caspar wanted to speak with him.

"IT'S KIND OF IMPORTANT, TUBBY," JAKE LABREAU HAD said, so Tubby agreed to come right over.

He had not been shown any back ways to the management offices of Casino Mall Grandé so he went in the front like the rest of the tourists. The same gay, electronic, noisy scene was still playing. The patrons sitting at their machines looked interchangeable—a lot of faces telling one story. Tubby suddenly realized it wasn't Tijuana souvenir makers they reminded him of, it was rows of women in full dresses sitting astride sewing machines in a picture from the 1920s he had seen once upon a time. It was the same unnatural look of people mating with machines. Tubby pushed these disturbing thoughts aside, remembering the large check he had that morning deposited in his bank account. He tuned into the squeal of good fortune and the hilarity of free booze and smiled contentedly.

He went upstairs with long strides and approached the guard

by the door marked PRIVATE. The man made a call and pointed
Tubby through. Nicole came out of Jake's office to greet him. She
looked tremendous.

"Hello, lawyer man," she said. "You're meeting with Mr. Caspar today?"

"That's what I'm told," Tubby said, pleased.

"Maybe we could have a cup of coffee afterwards. I'll take you
to his office."

She took him around a corner and past a receptionist. She
tapped lightly on the open door and showed Tubby into Caspar's
opulent purple-and-black suite. The manager arose from behind
his shining desk and pointed Tubby to one of a pair of garish uphol-
stered chairs.

Nicole said, "I'll see you later," and winked and left, closing the
door as she went out.

Three squad cars raced by outside with sirens bleeping. Must
be a movie star in town.

Mr. Caspar looked friendly for a change. He came around his
desk and settled down with Tubby in the matching chair separated
by a low butler's table.

"You did well the other night, am I right?"

"Very well. It was unreal." Tubby was beginning to suspect that
there was more to his good fortune than pure luck.

"Good. You wanna smoke?" Caspar lifted the lid of a silver box
on the table and helped himself to a cigar. Tubby said no, thanks.

"Let's see if your luck still holds." Caspar fanned a deck of
Casino Mall Grandé playing cards on the table's surface.

"Hundred dollars—cut you for high card," Caspar said.

"Okay," Tubby said. This must be how gamblers did business.

"You first," Caspar directed.

Tubby flipped a card. It was a jack.

Caspar stared at Tubby, smiling his mirthless smile. Without
looking down he turned over a ten.

"You win," he said.

He pulled a roll from his pants pocket and peeled off a hundred-dollar bill.

"Hey, that's okay," Tubby said.

"No, take it," Caspar insisted. "A bet's a bet."

Tubby took the money. He was starting to like this job.

"They call you Tubby?" Caspar asked, inhaling his cigarette.

"Yeah."

"What's that from?"

"It's just a nickname I picked up in high school. I was pretty big. I wrestled and played some ball."

"It's a funny name." The way Caspar said it, it didn't sound funny.

"Yeah."

Caspar smoked.

"We got an important job for you, Dubonnet. We're opening up a sidewalk café outside, and we want to sell beer, wine, and mixed drinks, of course. We'd like you to research that for us. See what we have to do to get our liquor license in place. Do you think you could handle that?"

"That's all?"

"What do you mean, that's all? Liquor is a big deal. I want you to spend some time on it. Do it right."

"Why, sure," Tubby said. This could be a couple of $2,000 days.

"We expect you to be reliable and dependable."

Tubby nodded.

"One of the family. Like you said, client satisfaction comes first."

Tubby nodded.

"Okay, enjoy the casino. You'll like what we got going. Go see Nicole. She knows all about our alcohol permits. She'll get you started."

CITY OF BEADS   129

"I gotcha," Tubby said.

Caspar stood up. There were no *toujours amours* in parting. Passing the office receptionist, Tubby found his own way out.

He located Nicole in a conference room. Papers and blueprints were spread out on a long table. She was reading something, wearing glasses—which was news to Tubby. She folded up what she was working on and looked up at him.

"Ready to go to work?" she asked.

"Let's see what you got," he replied, and sat beside her.

She handed Tubby a folder. "Here are copies of all of our liquor permits. Take it with you. I think you're supposed to figure out if they cover a sidewalk café or if we need to go back to the Alcohol and Beverage Control Board."

"Easy enough," Tubby said. He put the folder in his briefcase and got up to leave.

Nicole blew him a kiss and waved goodbye. She must have forgotten about the coffee.

CHAPTER

Twenty-Two

PASTOR GREEN HAD PREACHED AT ST. MARY'S AMERICAN Baptist Church for only two years, and he didn't yet feel completely in charge of his small congregation. He knew that in the eyes of several of his older members he could probably never fill the shoes of Pastor Jefferson, who had spent over twenty years in the very same pulpit. And because he was barely thirty years old himself he was sometimes a little unsure of the counsel he offered when people came to him with troublesome problems about which he admittedly had no practical experience. It was the younger members of the congregation he felt were on his wavelength, and to whom he looked for support in the many difficult tasks of building a church.

He was especially pleased, therefore, when one of his most active young women, Tania Thompson, presented herself in the church office. After saying a polite hello she asked if he could spare a few minutes to talk.

"Why yes, sister. Please sit down." He bumped painfully against the corner of his desk in his haste to offer her a chair. "You don't have to ask. I'm never too busy to see you.

"Tell me," he said, returning to his side of the desk, but still standing in case she needed something. Water perhaps. A comforting word. "What brings you here today? No trouble in the choir, I hope."

Tania sang with the St. Mary's Heavenly Harmonettes, the church's renowned gospel messengers. Keeping its members from feuding was a constant and worrisome challenge for Pastor Green.

He was relieved when she said no.

"Something . . . personal . . . then?" he asked, dropping his voice and assuming a more serious expression.

"Yes, Pastor. Very personal. I have committed a great sin, and I need to feel right with the Lord."

"Please tell me what has happened," Pastor Green implored anxiously.

So Tania told him the astonishing story of how she had stalked Charlie Van Dyne and finally shot him down. As the tale unwound, Pastor Green's face underwent dramatic changes. From nods of benign understanding it transformed into genuine horror. By the end it had reshaped into something composed and somber, and, yes, pastoral.

"What possessed you, sister, to take this into your own hands?" he asked.

"I wanted justice to be done for once." Tania was crying. "I was sick and tired of seeing them get away with taking life, anybody's life they want to. I prayed about it hard, Pastor, and I thought it was right. But now I see that it was just revenge, not justice, I was after. And that makes it a sin, Pastor, doesn't it?"

"Before we go any further with this, Sister Thompson, we're going to pray about it. Come on, down on your knees with me." He came to her side, and together they knelt on the worn carpet of his study.

"Lord, You have heard this confession that Sister Thompson has made, and now we are kneeling before You, in Your holy house, to pray for forgiveness. Terrible deeds have been done and blood has been spilled. This innocent child has done the spilling. We know, Lord, that You are a jealous God, that vengeance is Yours, and not for us. Maybe, just maybe, You selected Sister Thompson as Your angel of vengeance. Verily we hope that is the case. If it was not your wish that she did what she did, then she is repenting, oh Lord, and asking Your forgiveness. Say you are repenting, Sister Thompson."

"I am repenting, dear God. Please forgive me."

"And Lord, if she was Your intended instrument of Holy Justice and Vengeance, then we hope and pray that You will lay your hand upon Sister Thompson and let her feel the healing balm of Your mercy so that she may know peace and wake up in the morning glad that she has done Your bidding. We pray for Your sweet mercy, dear Lord."

"I pray for your mercy, Lord."

"Forgiveness or mercy, either one, dear God, so that the child may be freed from her torment. Amen."

"Amen."

Tania gave the pastor a hug and then reached into her purse for a tissue to dry her eyes. Pastor Green helped her up.

"The Lord never leaves you, sister," he said, guiding her back to her chair.

"Thank you so much, Pastor. I feel a great deal better than when I came in."

"Well, sister, that's why I am here." Pastor Green looked serious, but inside he was bursting with power and joy.

"There is something else I need to tell you," Tania said.

"You might as well go ahead and tell it all."

"Some men have tried to hurt me. They came into my home and tried to kill me. I got away, but they tore up my place something awful."

"Are you in danger?"

"I suppose so, Pastor, but that's not what I need your advice with."

"Go ahead."

"A man helped me. He was a stranger, but he took me in and

hid me. He even let me stay at his house until I was ready to go back home. I think maybe I fell in love with him a little."

"That's understandable, sister," the pastor said, though he was greatly disappointed.

"Thing is," Tania said, "he's white. That runs against my principles."

The pastor, too, was disturbed, and he hemmed and hawed a minute to get his emotions in line and his thoughts organized.

"This is not something we would normally approve of," he said slowly. His voice had gotten deeper. "It makes for great difficulties. Many a white man has mistreated the black woman. On the other hand, where people truly care about each other there is no black or white."

"He's a lawyer," Tania said mournfully.

"More serious than I had feared. This may be very, very hard for the Lord to understand and forgive," the pastor said solemnly. "You need to be very careful, very careful indeed. Pray about this one, sister. Don't ever forget to pray."

"I won't ever forget that, Pastor."

"And as long as he's a lawyer, get some help from him. You're probably going to need some help to stay out of serious trouble over this whole mess."

"He's already done a lot."

"Well, let him help you some more. If he doesn't we've got some good African-American lawyers, too. You got to use these people sometimes. Even though they may work for Caesar. Sometimes God's children need a lawyer's help so they can stay free to do the Lord's work."

CHAPTER
Twenty-Three

YOU SHOULD NEVER BE IN A HURRY AT ANTOINE'S. LET the waiters hurry. There are enough of them. Tubby's choice was Joe Arnado. He always called Joe ahead of time to make a reservation, and he always liked the table he got. The other thing he liked about Joe was his utter unpretentiousness. While the menu offered *"Huîtres,"* from Joe you got:

"The oysters are nice today, Mr. Dubonnet. You can get them raw, fried, or some Rockefeller. Any way you like. And the crabmeat is a good starter. We got it lump or with a little étouffée sauce, or we can make it up in a crab cake. However you like it."

Tubby was especially fond of Antoine's appetizers. He loved the Oysters Foch, oysters large and plump covered in a rich brown gravy laced with wine. And he liked the crisp shrimp fritters. He liked the desserts. If he had the time and the appetite, the baked Alaska, its crisp meringue melting with the ice cream, was the stuff of dreams. But best of all was the service. There always seemed to be approximately as many vintage Italian attendants for each guest as there were pieces of silverware beside his plate.

Judge Hughes was Tubby's guest today. Their friendship went back to law school. When Alvin Hughes decided to become one of the first blacks to run for a judgeship on the Civil District Court, Tubby had been one of his campaign advisors in what became a locally historic election. Now the roles were reversed, and Tubby banked on the advice the judge so freely gave. For example:

"I suggest you get the flounder," the judge advised. "I had it last week and it was very, very good."

"I was thinking about the soft-shell crabs, but maybe I'll go with the flounder."

Arnado appeared at the table, trailing servants with water pitchers. He was a big man and had to stoop to take orders. He had put two kids through Loyola on Antoine's tips.

"You gentlemen know what entrées you want yet?"

"Flounder for me, Joe, and could you bring some more of these potato crisps while we wait?"

"Surely. And you, Judge?"

"Soft-shell crabs, lightly grilled, and pick us out some pretty good wine, please. Mr. Dubonnet is paying."

"Okay. The crabs are real big, real fresh today. How about some Pouilly-Fuissé, Mr. Dubonnet?"

The judge grinned, Tubby nodded, and Joe was gone.

"You don't have to rush back, do you?" Tubby asked.

"Oh, no. I'm done for the day. I had, I think, sixty-three rules on my docket this morning. That's it for me. Anybody else comes in Mrs. Dobbs will direct to the duty judge."

"I don't see how you keep up with all your cases."

"Keeping up with the cases is the lawyer's job. I just decide them. And I've got good clerks. They research everything and tell me what to do. I could handle the job drunk." That was baloney, Tubby knew. Judge Hughes got reversed less on appeal than just about any other judge in the city.

"You had any interesting cases lately?" Tubby asked.

"I had one last week where the lawyer was struck dumb. I'm not kidding. You know Morey Goldfine?"

"Sure I do. He's a royal pain in the ass. Good litigator, I guess, if you like obnoxious. He sort of got the better of me in a case by going behind my back to Judge Coker. At least I think he did."

"Then you'll like this. You know how excited he gets?"

"He's always excited. He's full of hot air." Tubby was down on Morey Goldfine.

"Yeah, right. So he's before me with a summary judgment motion, and Ralph Pettus is on the other side. Every time Pettus speaks, Morey is on his feet interrupting. I mean he's not even objecting, he's just being rude. I told him to stop it maybe three times, but he can't quit. He's building up steam. His face gets all red and his cheeks are pooching out."

Judge Hughes tried to do an imitation, and Tubby started laughing.

"Pettus is just laying out his argument," the judge resumed, "but I'm watching Morey get ready to explode. Finally he can't take it no more. He jumps up, scattering his notes everywhere, and he turns around to look at me with his arms spread out like he's gonna sing and his big mouth wide open. Then he sees I got my hand out like this." Judge Hughes held up his palm like a cop stopping traffic. "He tries to stop himself, and his face, like, convulses. I tell him to sit down, but he starts pounding himself on the chest. I think he gave himself a heart attack or something. I had to recess court and let him go sit in my chambers for a few minutes. Mrs. Dobbs called a doctor for him. When Morey came out he literally couldn't talk. He'd locked up his larynx."

"Well deserved," Tubby said. "So what did you do?"

"I ruled against him and called the next case."

Tubby laughed some more.

"I hear he's okay now," the judge added.

They were surrounded by waiters bringing food and wine. The crew departed as quickly as it had arrived, and fine dining commenced.

"I haven't seen you around the courthouse lately," the judge observed, before he put away a steamy bite of crab, sautéed in garlic butter.

"I haven't had to go. I've been down to Criminal Court though."

"What you got?"

"Oh, a kid accused of stealing a motorcycle. He didn't do it, but I can't seem to get any consideration out of the district attorney."

"They hear about innocent perpetrators all the time."

"I know, but this kid is truly innocent."

"Who's your judge?"

"Calabrissi."

"He's running for reelection."

"So what?"

"Think about it." The judge patted his lips with his napkin.

"You're probably right." Tubby sighed.

"So how's your love life?"

"Well, at least I have one," Tubby said.

"Really? Tell me more." The judge broke off a piece of French bread to mop up some melted butter.

"There's a beautiful woman interested in me. She's got all her teeth, a good job, everything a man could want."

"Attaboy. She met your daughters yet?"

"No, we're not exactly that far along."

They ate in silence for a minute.

"Tubby, correct me if I'm wrong, but you don't seem to be as excited about this relationship as would seem to be appropriate for a man of your dubious attractiveness and advancing years."

"You got that right. The thing is . . . well, this is a little bit of a delicate topic. There's another lady I am also sort of interested in."

"Aha," the judge said encouragingly.

"The thing is, the other lady is black."

"Oh, ho." The judge laughed loudly enough to startle other diners in the vicinity. "You have tasted the famous . . ."

"Please don't say brown sugar," Tubby interrupted.

"I was going to say milk chocolate," Hughes concluded benignly.

"This is serious, Al. It's a new thing for me, and for her, too. And I haven't tasted anything yet."

"Tubby, why should it make the slightest difference what her race is?"

"It doesn't, so far. But if we get to know each other better I just wonder if, I don't know, certain biases might come out."

"Son, the thing to do is to get those biases to march right out, if you got 'em, and then get rid of them. Don't be a chicken about this."

"What if it was your daughter?"

"To be honest, I'd rather she marry a black man because it would be easier all around. But the main thing is for her to marry a good man. You should try harder to be happy, Tubby. You worry too much. Follow your heart."

"I hear you," Tubby said.

"Also, I certainly understand your dilemma. Since so many of your people have moved out of town, there are not that many white girls around to pick from anymore."

"Sad, but true," Tubby said.

CHAPTER

Twenty-Four

TUBBY CALLED CHERRYLYNN TO GET HIS MESSAGES. There weren't many. His client Adrian, also known as Monster Mudbug, had called. Also, one Bijan Botaswati had left a number.

"It's pretty interesting about him, boss. I didn't do too well at the Levee Board," she reported tentatively.

"Why not? What happened?"

"Well, it took a long time to find someone to help me. Then I didn't know the correct description of the property where any of the companies on the list were. They have some big maps, and one man helped me find the areas I was interested in. Did you know Bayou Disposal is close to Mr. Aucoin's shop, Export Products?"

"I hadn't thought about it."

"Well, it is. Anyway, I ran out of time, and I have to go back, but he did help me figure out that there's another company on Twink Beekman's list that leases a place right next to Bayou Disposal."

"What's that?"

"It's called Multitronica, and guess what."

"What?"

"I just checked with the corporations division of the secretary of state, and the incorporator of Multitronica is also Bijan Botaswati."

"Interesting."

"Yeah, and I found out that Cargo Planners has closed up shop. The man told me that Bayou Disposal is still in business, but it has

moved somewhere. They are no longer there. They both assigned
their leases to a company called Ship Ahoy."

"Let me guess."

"Yes sir. Its incorporator is Mr. Botaswati. What does it mean?"

"It probably means he's a nominee for other people who don't
want their names known."

"Why would he let them use his name?"

"'They have looked each other between the eyes, and
there they have found no fault. They have taken the Oath of the
Brother-in-Blood on leavened bread and salt,'" Tubby said mildly.
"Kipling."

"Right, boss," Cherrylynn said, and hung up.

TUBBY CALLED TWINK BEEKMAN AND TOLD HIM WHAT
little he had learned and the interesting coincidence that a French
Quarter tavern keeper and souvenir purveyor seemed strangely involved with several possible river polluters. Twink found it all most
suspicious and, hinting at dark conspiracies, said he would try to locate where the nefarious Bayou Disposal had disappeared to.

Nothing like a mystery to get the juices flowing. Tubby poked
Bijan Botaswati's number into the phone, and a female answered,
"Orleans Records, Tapes, and T-Shirts, Julie speaking. May I help
you?"

Tubby asked for Mr. Botaswati. Julie wanted to know who was
calling, and he told her.

In a minute a thickly accented voice said, "Hello."

"Mr. Botaswati?"

"Yes."

"My name is Tubby Dubonnet, and I'm an attorney." Tubby
generally called himself a lawyer, like to regular people and juries,
but to foreigners or someone from California he always said attor-

ney. "I have an important proposition to discuss with you. I have clients in Lahore who have asked me to contact you."

"Who are these clients?"

"I am afraid I cannot tell you that on the telephone, but I think you would find the proposition very intriguing. It involves a lot of money. I suggest that we meet."

"Okay. I can meet with you. When?"

"The sooner the better."

"You could come here to my shop right now. There is a place we can talk."

"Very good," Tubby said. He got the address on Decatur Street and hung up the phone. What did he think he was doing? Tubby asked himself—why go around meddling in the affairs of a local businessman who was, no doubt, entitled to his little secrets? Because, at that moment, a walk to the French Quarter struck him as much more interesting than looking into the alcoholic beverage permits of Casino Mall Grandé.

He noticed the strand of glass beads where he had tossed them on his desk. Idly, he draped them over the shade of his lamp. They came alive and sent blue flashes around the room, so he left them there.

JULIE THE CLERK WAS WAITING ON A CREW OF CUSTOM-ers when Tubby walked in, big people in short pants buying New Orleans T-shirts for Mary and Ted and Aunt Rena back home in Ohio. He waited politely while she rang up her sale and got momentarily engrossed in a rack of postcards of semi-naked men and women in outrageous Mardi Gras masks posing on wrought-iron balconies and under famous French Quarter street signs.

"May I help you?" Julie asked brightly.

"I talked to you earlier. I'm Mr. Dubonnet, and I'm here to see Mr. Botaswati."

She told him to wait a moment please, and she relayed the message on a telephone.

"He'll be right here. Can I show you anything while you wait?"

He stared at a glass case full of rubber sex toys, joke condoms, a baseball cap with a foam alligator on top, a whole wall of ceramic clown faces.

"No, I think I'll just browse. Does Mr. Botaswati own many shops?"

"Oh, yes sir. He owns another T-shirt shop on Canal Street, and a bar called The Hard Rider on Burgundy, and . . ."

A tall, very erect, dark-skinned man entered through the plastic strips that took the place of a door. He had a plentiful mustache and very intense eyebrows and gave the impression of a senior military officer in a colonial horse cavalry.

"Yes, and you are Mr. Dubonnet?" he asked.

"Mr. Botaswati." Tubby extended his hand, and Mr. Botaswati gave it a limp shake.

"This way, please." He led the way around the curtain to the back of the store. "You will watch the front?" he asked Julie, and she said she would.

The office was functional. More room was given to racks of clothes and cardboard boxes of merchandise than to the desk where Tubby and Botaswati talked.

"You said you had a proposition for me," the host began.

"Are you the same Bijan Botaswati who owns Bayou Disposal?" Tubby asked.

Botaswati looked confused. "I have many interests," he said. "I could not tell you if that is one or not."

"I believe it is one."

"So what?" Botaswati asked, and shrugged.

"I have been asked to bring a lawsuit to have Bayou Disposal stop dumping chemicals into the river."

"What are you talking about?" Botaswati was growing agitated. "What does this have to do with clients of yours in Lahore?"

"Nothing," Tubby said. "I made them up. I wanted to meet the man responsible for these companies that are possibly polluting the river."

"You made them up? Fantastic. You should come in my store with such a trick. Responsible? I am responsible for nothing. This disposal company is somebody else's concern. It does not even have a lease anymore on the river. It is gone. And I want you gone from my store."

"It is your concern if it has violated any laws. If someone else truly owns the company, you should tell me and protect yourself."

"I will tell you nothing. These are big people. Very much bigger than you. Now you get out of my shop." He stood up and gestured for Tubby to do the same.

He clucked and fretted until Tubby was outside on the sidewalk. Julie smiled and waved goodbye. She started to tell him to Have a Nice Day, but her boss growled at her and she shut up.

CHAPTER

Twenty-Five

BROUSSARD LOOKED AT HIS BIG HANDS, OR OUT THE window, or at the painting on the wall behind Tubby's head. Everywhere but at Tubby. He had on baggy jeans, rough leather work boots, and he kept nervously rolling and unrolling the sleeves of his blue work shirt, exposing a tattoo of a coiled dragon. He had his hair pulled back in a ponytail, though he looked close to Tubby's age. He had come to Tubby's office at Edith Aucoin's request, bringing with him copies of the last contracts of Export Products. Tubby was trying to find out the status of each job, and when it would be over with, but it was slow going.

"You were Mr. Aucoin's foreman, right?"

"Yes, sir," Broussard said to the painting, in careful, Cajun-spiced American.

"Are you still keeping a full crew working?"

"No. Down to two."

"Are you going to be able to finish up each of these jobs?"

"Oh sure. It's hard, but we're gon' do it."

"Okay, like this one—'Shipment fifty thousand gallons, f.o.b. San Salvador.' When will that be finished?"

"Monday or Tuesday, latest."

"Who is picking up the barge?"

"Towboat."

"What company?"

"Could be any company."

"How do you know which one?"

"Whichever shows up."

"How do you know they're entitled to take the oil?"

"Why else would dey want it?"

It took Tubby about an hour to realize that he really did not care how the business operated because it would be wrapped up in a week or so and Broussard had it under control. He sent the foreman on his way.

Fifteen minutes later, while he was organizing the papers on his desk, Cherrylynn told him the security man downstairs wanted to speak with him urgently. He picked up the phone.

"Mr. Dubonnet?"

"Yes, Carl. What is it?"

"There was some kind of workman asking where your office was earlier. Did he come to see you?"

"Yes."

"I thought you ought to know he's been shot right here in the elevator."

"What?"

"Yes, sir. Shot dead. We got the elevators blocked down here. The police are on the way over."

"I'll be right down."

SIRENS WERE GOING OFF IN THE ELEVATOR HALL, AND it took a minute to ascertain that everything but the freight elevator had been shut off. It finally answered Tubby's insistent summons, and he descended to the first floor. When he stepped out he found that he was within the area cordoned off by the —building's security people, who were holding back a growing crowd of secretaries, lawyers, and accountants all trying to get to their offices.

The doors of all the cars gaped open, and the computer voice in each one repeated mindlessly, over and over, "Do not be alarmed. Service is temporarily interrupted. It will be restored shortly. Do not be alarmed. . . ."

Carl, the guard he said hello to each morning, was standing in front of one of the cars. He stepped aside to give Tubby a look.

Broussard was sitting against the polished walnut back wall of the car with his legs spread out in front of him. There was a small red hole in his left temple, and his eyes stared at the ceiling as if still avoiding human contact. The blood on his shoulder and here and there around the elevator still glistened.

"Jesus," Tubby said.

"The first lady who saw him fainted," Carl said. "She's in the office. The elevator went up and down a couple more times before we stopped it. We got reports from every floor in the building. I think there's quite a few people upstairs who are gonna be afraid to ride the elevator again."

"Stand back." He heard behind him the first policemen coming onto the scene. He spotted Kathy Jeansonne trying to get through the security crew. He could see Detective Kronke bringing up the rear.

Here we go again, he thought.

CHAPTER

Twenty-Six

IT WAS LATE WHEN TUBBY GOT BACK TO THE OFFICE. Just to get it over with, and to make Detective Kronke happy, he had gone down to the police station and had recounted, in numbing detail, everything Broussard had said during his visit to the office. Kronke had thought it all quite peculiar, but he had treated Tubby with respect.

He was glad, however, that he had decided against going straight home, because Tania called. Cherrylynn asked her to wait while she saw if he was in, but he immediately picked up the phone. She said she wanted to talk to him in person. He said not at the office, and after they tossed some ideas back and forth they settled on Mike's Bar.

As he was saying goodbye to Cherrylynn, Twink Beekman also checked in. When Tubby's daughters were little and asked him what he did for a living, Tubby said, "I just talk on the phone." This was one of those days when he wished it were true.

"I've tracked down Bayou Disposal, Mr. D. They've set up shop on Highway 39 way out past Chalmette. I think it's all the way into Plaquemines Parish."

"How'd you find that out?"

"I just picked up the phone and called their number in the phone book."

"Oh, good thinking."

"I'm going to drive down there myself. Maybe take Debbie. We'll check it out."

"Just the two of you?"

"Sure, Mr. D. Listen, I have a fiancée and everything. I'll be on good behavior."

"I wasn't thinking about that, Twink. I was thinking it might be a little dangerous. You know, out in the parish people don't like investigators snooping around."

"Have no fear. I'll take care of everything."

"I'm sure you can, Twink. Still, I'd like to send one of my associates along with you. I'd feel better."

"That's fine, too. You're the lawyer."

And the father, you dipstick, Tubby thought to himself.

TANIA ARRIVED AT MIKE'S BEFORE TUBBY DID AND SHE was greeted warmly by Mr. Mike. He didn't actually get up from his chair, but he made his nephew get up and give her his seat at Mike's table, where a couple of sportsmen were cutting for high card.

"Look who's here," he said. "Little Orphan Annie in from the cold again."

"I brought back your wife's coat," she said. "I had it cleaned."

"You should have kept it. It looks a lot better on you. So who's chasing you this time?"

"Nobody, I hope. I'm supposed to meet Mr. Dubonnet here."

"Tubby's coming over? Good, 'cause I need to speak to him. How about a drink? You want something to drink?"

She said no, but finally settled on a rum and Coke because it was a special occasion, Mr. Mike said.

Tubby got buzzed in and got a loud reception from Mr. Mike, too. He was served the same drink, and an earful from Mr. Mike. It seems Ernie had been found, hiding out in a "cabana," Mr. Mike said, in the Atchafalaya swamp. And guess what! The whole $55,000 had gone into video poker. Who would think it was possible to lose that much. The cousins were putting Ernie to work to pay Mike back, but that would take years. What a family.

Finally Tubby was permitted to adjourn with Tania to a table in the corner where they could talk.

"It's nice to see you again," Tubby said, sipping his fizzy drink. He put his elbows on the table and leaned a little closer to her. He did not feel like telling her about the shooting in his building.

"Yes, it's nice to see you," she said.

"You left my house in rather a hurry."

"I had to get back to work, and I knew eventually I had to face up to my own house again."

"Have you got things straightened up?"

"Pretty much. There were some important things I had to throw away. You musn't get too attached to things."

"There hasn't been any further trouble? No threats?"

"No, but I did think a car was following me yesterday when I drove home from work."

"What do you have that these guys want?"

She took her time. "You said once you were not my lawyer, but I wonder if I can hire you to help me."

"I suppose so," Tubby said. "Why don't you tell me what the trouble is."

"How much do you charge?"

"You want to be serious about this?"

She nodded.

"How about five dollars? And for that you can tell me what is going on with you. After that I'll decide if I need to charge you more."

"Very well." She fished around in her purse and took out a $10 bill, which she put on the table.

"I don't have a five," she said.

"We can make change later. So tell me."

While Tubby finished his drink in silence, she told him. She covered the murder of her brother, her identification of Charlie Van Dyne's house, her nights on patrol, and the way she had fired her brother's pistol at the Bouligny Steak House.

Tubby was shocked, and strangely fascinated.

"I know the name Van Dyne" was all he could think of to say. "He sold some bad drugs to a man named Jerome Rasheed Cook."

Tania just stared at her hands. They were picking apart the wet napkin under her glass.

"Do you actually feel what you did was right?" Tubby asked.

"I feel it was right." Tania looked up. "But I think it was wrong, if that makes sense. I'm still praying about it."

"These men are after you for what? To pay you back for what you did?" He couldn't quite bring himself to say "for shooting a man dead."

"Yes, I think so."

"The police haven't shown any interest in you?"

"None at all."

"I think I'm going to keep the whole ten dollars. You want another drink?"

Tania said no.

"Me neither," Tubby said. "Okay. Let me think about this a minute."

God, what an incredible situation. Tubby searched his memory for a point of reference in the rules of professional conduct. He was familiar with them, but only the big rules, like zealously representing your client and keeping her confidences, came to mind. His thought process kept getting knocked off track by aftershocks from the revelation that pretty, petite, pious Tania could actually shoot a man. Premeditated. At close range.

"Was it, uh, hard for you to pull the trigger when he turned around and looked at you?"

"I'd be lying if I said it was hard. It scared me because it was so easy. I'm sad that I have to carry it around with me for the rest of my life. I've been talking to the minister at my church about it."

"You're not planning to shoot anybody else, are you?"

"No," she said simply.

"That's good," Tubby said.

"It felt like something or someone was guiding my hand. Now that it's done, that power isn't there anymore. I'm back to being me."

"It wouldn't be proper for me to help you conceal your crime, but I'm curious. What did you do with the gun?"

"I threw it in the trash, and the garbage men took it away."

"Oh. What do you want me to do?"

"I want you to defend me if I'm caught."

"I'll certainly do that."

"Or if I decide to turn myself in to the police."

"I would defend you then, too. But my job isn't to tell you whether or not to turn yourself in."

"I understand that."

"While you think about it, I'd say you have bigger problems, like staying alive. Is there any reason to think there won't be more attempts on your life?"

"Well, I did hurt one of the men pretty bad, I think. I believe they will come back after me, and I won't lie, I'm very scared."

"Do you have any idea who they are?"

"I think their names are Coco and Hambone, but they work for someone else."

"Do you know who that someone else is?"

"I wish I did. When the people talked about 'the man,' they were talking about Charlie Van Dyne. Everybody in the neighborhood thought he was like the godfather, you know. I haven't any idea who is above him."

"Did you ever think, Tania, that you might have been wrong? That Mr. Van Dyne might not have been the godfather at all? I mean, I have heard from someone else that he was involved in dealing drugs, so he probably was. But to kill him? Do you ever think that maybe he didn't deserve that?"

"No, I didn't really ever think that. People knew it was him. The folks in my neighborhood are wrong sometimes, but not about things like that. They are very streetwise. He was the man who killed my brother. And you may not understand what I'm saying, but I was guided to him."

"Fine. As long as you're not guided to anybody else. I'll be your lawyer, but it won't be much of a job right now. You call me if you need me. If you find out anything about who Charlie Van Dyne reported to, let me know. And I'll ask around, too."

"Okay."

They both stared at their glasses, watching the ice melt.

"I was always a good girl," Tania said. "I always tried to please my mama and papa, and do the right things. I tried hard to make a success of myself."

"I understand," Tubby said.

"I just want to get my life back on track."

"I can't forgive you, Tania. That's not in my department."

"I know that," she said, and dabbed at her eyes with a tissue wrapped around her finger. "Only Jesus can."

Tubby paid at the bar.

TUBBY ARRIVED AT HIS OFFICE EARLY THE NEXT MORNing, even before Cherrylynn. An acquaintance of his, Nick Nicarro, also known as the Newsman, was on the job early, and Tubby wanted to talk to him on the phone. Nick sold newspapers, magazines, racing forms, and dirty books in the French Quarter, and he tried to read everything that passed through his store. Nick's mind was a biological filing cabinet of the grotesque, the bizarre, and the outrageously criminal. He digested police stories by the ream and could relate the facts of beheadings, dismemberments, and mutilations from North Carolina to Oregon. He especially liked stories with a local twist, and he could tell you plenty about New Orleans sickos.

Nick knew his underworld. He did not, however, have much of a file on Charlie Van Dyne.

"The guy who got killed at Bouligny's Steak House?" he asked.

"The same," Tubby said.

"I seem to think like he hangs around with the wrong crowd."

"You mean like crooks?"

"Oh, no. I think he's connected with a lot of cops. He's some kind of upright citizen."

"I heard he had street pushers working for him."

"I heard the same," Nick said.

"Any idea who Charlie worked for? I mean, he couldn't have been the top of the heap."

"Top of the heap? There's still plenty of dope on the streets, right. Nobody ever gets to the top of the heap. Van Dyne worked for somebody, sure. It could be any one of three or four different people."

"You're not sure which?"

"I just know *almost* everything, Tubby. I ain't God."

"Yeah, but you're the smartest guy in the world, Nick, when it comes to getting the real nitty-gritty on crime. We all know that."

Nick was flattered. "Well, maybe I can ask around and turn something up. If I do, I'll call you."

"I'd appreciate it. You're a pal."

"Yeah, but you don't ever come by, Tubby. I'm forgetting what you look like. You getting any thinner?"

"Whatcha mean? I'm in great shape."

"Come by the store so I can admire you then. We got some real good exercise books you might like. Richard Simmons, for example, would be perfect for you."

"Give me a break."

"I'm just thinking about your health."

"You and everybody else. I'm in the prime of life."

"Anybody breathing can say that. Hey, I got a customer. I'll call you if I find something."

"See you," Tubby said.

After he hung up, Tubby paused to look out his window at the city and river below him. A long yellow tanker with the name STOLT painted in huge letters along its length was being turned in the river and pushed toward a wharf by three tugboats. From up here, this rearrangement of massive tonnage against a powerful current looked as effortless as a twig drifting around in a stream. The beads hanging from his desk lamp captured the day's early sunshine.

CHAPTER

Twenty-Seven

TUBBY QUICKLY TIRED OF THE LIQUOR LICENSE PROJ-
ect. This was not his strong suit, but from what he could see the
casino had so many permits to sell alcoholic beverages that Leo
could open up twenty sidewalk cafés and hang three more off the
balcony and still be legal. Surely there was more to the assignment
than this. His conscience would bother him if he billed for more
than a day's work. His original concept had been to bill for lots of
days' work. He laid the file aside with a dejected shake of his head
and called up Monster Mudbug.

"Adrian," he said. "Is your old man still a poll watcher? Is he
still active in the Old Regulated Democrats?"

"I think so," Adrian said. "He goes to a lot of meetings. I don't
know what they're for."

"I think there's something you need to check out with your
dad."

"Okay," Adrian said.

"Go tell him the judge in your case is Calabrissi. Ask him has
he made any contributions to the judge's reelection effort. Ask him
who the Old Regulateds are supporting."

"He's watching TV in the living room. You want me to go ask
him now?"

"No. I don't even want to know the answers. Just lay it out for
him, and see if he can't think of something to do about your situation."

"Okay, Mr. Tubby. Whatever you say. Sounds like one of them New Orleans kinda things to me."

"Yeah, you're right, Adrian. I'll see you in court."

There was rarely a shortage of things for Tubby to do in the office. He did, however, sometimes complete all of the interesting tasks he could think of and had to decide which boring or difficult project to resurrect from the bottom of the heap. He pulled open his desk drawer, idly hoping for a distraction. He found some old parking receipts and a letter he had never mailed to his ex-wife, but nothing to do. Reluctantly he scanned the various piles of files on the couch and floor, and his eyes stopped at the expandable brown folder that was labeled "Save Our River." Unexciting though the matter might be, it was at least a file he had not yet read. He got up and brought it over to his desk, emptied its contents, and sorted the folders into neat stacks. Then he sat down to digest.

Ten minutes into it he had a pretty good idea about what the students were up to. In commendably organized fashion, they had broken the Orleans Parish riverfront, together with the Industrial Canal, the Harvey Canal, and the Intracoastal Waterway as far as the Gulf Outlet, into sections, and had created an "inventory" of all the shippers, warehousers, grain elevators, and stevedores that conducted their dirty and venerable businesses there. Just producing the list must have required a great amount of labor. It was all stored on a computer and updated every six months. Apparently someone had compiled descriptions of what each company did, and scored its "hazard potential," but Tubby's file contained only the summaries, not the volumes of lists and raw data.

Then there were folders marked "Hot Spots" and "Investigation Needed." Tubby began reading these reports carefully. They weren't boring.

Thirty minutes later he found the following, on smudged paper, like it had been typed up in a place where there was a lot of sweat and grime.

I took the following statement from Mr. Potter Aucoin at Export Products on the Napoleon Avenue wharf on May the 13th.

Signed: Kelly Stuveysant, "The Environment and You 203." Professor: Mr. Strapp.

My name is Potter Aucoin, and on January 5 and again on about January 17 I observed some workmen from Bayou Disposal run a four-inch hose from one of their red trucks out of their yard and down the riverbank to where there are trees growing out of the water. I was concerned that they might be crossing my property, but I saw that they were crossing the lot next to mine. It looked like the hose filled up, but I couldn't definitely see anything going into the river because the nozzle of the hose was under the water. After approximately fifteen minutes the men checked the truck from a hatch on the top and then pulled the hose back to their yard. I have no idea what they were draining into the river. I did not talk to any of the workmen. No one else was with me when I saw this. It was probably nothing. It is not really my business.

Potter Aucoin

Tubby sat back in shock. It was so unlike Potter to care dippity-do about river pollution.

He called Debbie's apartment. No answer. He called Twink Beekman, but the phone just rang. He called Raisin, and got Melinda, the nurse.

"No, he's not here, Tubby. He *said* he was driving down to Plaquemines Parish. I thought he said he was going with one of your daughters." Tubby detected the small blossom of suspicion in Melinda's voice.

"That's right," he said quickly. "I was just trying to get them before they left."

"Well, you missed them by an hour. He didn't say when he'd be back," she said flatly.

"Would you ask him to call me right away when you hear from him?"

She said she would.

Tubby called Botaswati's T-shirt shop, and his bar. Both places gave him the same story. Not here. The bartender was more direct.

"He say not to talk to you," and she hung up.

There was nothing to do but fidget. He plowed into his stack of deadly files, killing the hours till he heard from someone.

CHAPTER
Twenty-Eight

"I'M NOT SURE WHICH WAY WE GO HERE," TWINK SAID.
He and Debbie were driving somewhere south of New Orleans on
an old concrete highway fringed with green slime and muddy road
litter. Black swamp, dense with crooked trees, elephant ears, and
jagged palmettos, came up to the shoulders. An occasional high
spot provided enough spongy ground for a seedy roadside tavern
or a heap of rusty oilfield drilling pipe. Their bumpy path kept
forking, with the right hand curving generally toward the Mississippi River and the left roughly in the direction of the man-made
Gulf Outlet, a Corps of Engineers boondoggle that was fast swallowing up what was left of the marsh. Debbie had a map, but none
of these details seemed to be on it.

"I think we should go that way," she said, pointing westward,
"and stay as close to the river levee as possible. That way we know
we can't get too lost."

"Are we there yet?" Raisin asked from the backseat. Tubby's
associate had been napping, and snoring gently, ever since their
journey had begun.

"Not yet, Mr. Partlow," Twink said. "But we should be getting
close." Raisin sat up and rubbed his eyes.

"You'll know you went too far if you get to the end of the road,"
Raisin said, yawning. On this bank of the river, the end of the line
was the courthouse and jail in Pointe à la Hache. The final thirty
miles of Louisiana extending past these weathered and humble

stone buildings into the Gulf of Mexico were accessible only by boat, a small boat at that.

"Great navigating," Twink commented. His bright red Chevy Blazer hopped along the uneven concrete. "Huey Long must have built this road."

"Or Leander Perez. My dad tells me he used to be the political kingpin down here."

Twink checked his watch. It was about three o'clock.

"I'd sure hate to get caught down here after dark," he said. Shadows from the oak trees draped in Spanish moss crowded the road.

Debbie nodded, but actually the prospect didn't frighten her. She had been boating and camping in remote places like this many times. It had usually been with her dad, however, and he had usually known where they were, or said he did.

After rocking along a few more miles the road came out into the light and regained the levee, the tall, grass-covered ridge that forced the river to stay in its channel. The highway traveled along its base, and Debbie pointed out the radio towers of a ship overtaking them, a surprising optical reminder that the surface of the river was at least five feet higher than the roof of the Blazer.

They passed square freshwater ponds on the left side of the road, and a sign, PARISH CRAWFISH FARMS, explained what they were. They passed a miniature industrial complex with shiny chrome pipes that apparently existed to pump something gaseous in or out of vessels berthed in the river. Then they went by a cattle farm with a couple of buffalo mixed in. Finally Debbie spotted a painted metal sign to Bayou Disposal.

An arrow pointed down a shell road away from the levee, and, after exchanging a look with Debbie, Twink turned the Blazer down it. Gravel rattled under the floorboard. Soon they were out of sight of the levee, and after skidding around a turn or two they found the entrance to Bayou Disposal, blocked by a new chain-link fence and a wooden guard shack.

Twink eased the Blazer up to the gate in the fence. Beyond it they could see a small fleet of red tanker trucks parked in a row beside a mobile home, apparently the office, which was mounted on concrete blocks. There were a couple of men in the distance working around the trucks, but no other visible activity.

A young man who needed a shave, wearing a brown jacket with a "Security Patrol" patch on the shoulder, leaned out the window of the guard booth.

"Can I help you?" he called.

Twink rolled down his window. "Is the office open?" he asked.

"Not really," the young man said. "Who are you looking for?"

"The manager," Twink said.

"Joel Prouix?"

Twink had no idea, but he said, "Yes."

"He's not here today."

"Well, is there anybody else in the office?"

"I'll call and see. What are your names?"

"My name's Beekman. What's all the security for?"

"Oh, we've had a little trouble lately with vandalism." The guard pulled his head back inside.

In a moment he poked it out again.

"They asked what your business was."

"I'm from Tulane University in New Orleans. I just wanted to see how y'all were handling your operation."

The head disappeared again, then returned.

"They say for you to write a letter."

"We just want to meet the people. It won't take a minute."

"They say for you to go away," the guard reported a little more forcefully. "This is private property," he said, making it official.

"Let's go, Twink," Raisin said.

Twink was ready to argue with the guard some more, but Debbie poked him in the ribs with her finger, and he got the message.

He turned the Blazer around in the driveway, grumbling.

"Why don't we go down the road a little farther," Debbie said. "Maybe there are some neighbors or something we can ask about what goes on at this place."

"Okay," he muttered discontentedly. "Makes you think they're hiding something, doesn't it?" In the backseat, Raisin was beginning to pay attention.

Farther along the back road they encountered more crawfish ponds, serene in the afternoon sunlight. Looking closely, they could see tiny orange flags sticking out of the water in straight rows. In one of the ponds some people were lazily paddling a pirogue, checking things in the water.

"I think those are the markers for the traps," Debbie said.

"I thought crawfish grew wild in the swamps," Twink griped. "This looks more like agribusiness."

As they got closer they could see that the people in the boat were taking nets out of the water, emptying them, and tossing them back in. The people were wearing pointed hats, and the immediate image was of a rice paddy in Cambodia.

"It's like another world," Twink said.

LATER, WHEN RAISIN REPORTED TO TUBBY, HE DE-scribed it this way:

"We drive up to this metal packing shed. Some men are hanging out in the shade, but they all fade. A big, fat, muscular guy comes out of the shed to meet us. He's Vietnamese or something. He doesn't look that friendly to me, but your man Twink jumps out and says hi. The man grins and pulls out his cigarettes, so I know he's not going to start shooting.

"Twink goes, 'We're from New Orleans, and we're doing some

research about water pollution. We're here to save you. Tell us everything you know about Bayou Disposal.'"

"He said that?" Tubby interrupted.

"No, just words to that effect."

"Okay."

"Yeah, so the guy lets out a loud noise that sounds like 'Vark,' and that's when I got the idea he doesn't speak English. Then this second guy comes out of the shed, and he asks can he help us. Twink gives his speech again.

"'You with the government?' the man asks. A very good question—shows he's alert.

"'No,' Twink says. 'We're students at Tulane University. We're investigating complaints about the possible illegal dumping of chemicals into the water.' I don't say anything, even though I know this guy is thinking ol' Raisin doesn't look like any Tulane student.

"'We don' like Bayou Disposal,' says this fella, let's call him Vark.

"'Ah,' Twink said. 'Can you tell us why?'

"Vark is willing to talk. He invites us in. So we go. It's dark in there. They pack fish and it smells like it, but right then nothing much was going on. He sits us all down for a powwow on some wooden crates. He joins us and lights another cigarette. I hear little, uh, shuffling noises behind me, and what do I see when I look over my shoulder but that we are not alone. Like a dozen men have drifted out of the recesses of this place and are checking us out. They're dressed for work, white rubber boots, dirty jeans, army jackets, baseball caps, shaggy hair. They all got short black mustaches. I begin to wonder if I am going to fail at my job of protecting young Miss Dubonnet. They're not threatening, but they ain't friendly either. They're not showing much.

"'So,' Debbie begins, 'have you had a problem with Bayou Disposal?'

"Vark says, 'Maybe a month ago they come in here. Bring in lots of trucks. Since then, the crawfish no good.'

"'What do you mean, no good?' Twink asks.

"'No good. Stay small, shells soft, shells white. All fishermen around here, same problem. Can't sell. Man from Mulate's, big restaurant, always buy my crawfish. He say too small now.'"

"You do a good dialect," Tubby said.

"I'm just practicing," Raisin said. "I haven't quite got it yet. 'You connect this to Bayou Disposal?' Debbie asks.

"'Yes,' Vark says. 'They put something in the ground. It gets in the water.'

"'Have you told anybody about this?' Debbie asks.

"'No,' Vark says. 'Why? They got big men with guns,' he says.

"'Let us help you catch them,' Debbie says.

"Then they all started talking to each other in their language. I get none of this, but it gets loud. Then"—Raisin snapped his fingers—"they turn it off and start nodding like it's all settled.

"'What can you do for us?' Vark asks.

"'We can report this to the government,' your daughter says. 'We are going to bring a lawsuit against Bayou Disposal to make them pay for what they are doing. We will take statements from you. We can tell your story to the newspapers.'

"'How long all this take?' Vark wants to know.

"'That's hard to say,' Twink tells them. The government is big and slow, but he has a secret weapon—a great lawyer named Tubby Dubonnet has volunteered to help them. He's going to take everybody to court."

"Jesus," Tubby moaned.

"They didn't seem immediately impressed with your name. I do not think they could quite pronounce it. More discussion ensues. It gets noisy. One guy with real big callused hands, flat like a plank, makes a speech. Vark interprets. 'He say courts take a very long time. Big politicians decide what the courts say. These people want to know how long it will take.'

"Twink says he doesn't know. 'If we catch them in the act, maybe we can get an injunction. Maybe as soon as a month, or . . . maybe longer.'

"They look doubtful. More discussion. More speeches. Sounds like a whole violin section out of tune. And then here comes something that sounds familiar. Somebody says, 'Bin Minny.' And then, after that, nobody said anything for a full minute. Vark is so deep in thought he lets his cigarette burn down to his fingers and has to throw it down and stomp on it. He says, 'They want to take care of it without you. You no worry about it.'

"Twink was unhappy. 'How can we not worry about it? They're breaking the law,' but Vark is not impressed. 'Men all want to be in business again soon,' he says. End of conference.

"Very politely, they show us the way out. By which I mean they all followed us outside and made sure we got in the Blazer. They were passing around a pack of Marlboros and having a huddle with each other when we drove away."

"What do you make of that?" Tubby asked.

"That they're planning to take care of the problem in their own way."

"What was Debbie's reaction?"

"She said it was sad they were so suspicious of us. It was sad that these people are newcomers to our country, and they don't know how to go about getting things done."

"But they may know how," Tubby said.

"That's what I was thinking," Raisin said.

CHAPTER

Twenty-Nine

TUBBY WAS WAITING OUTSIDE DIXON HALL WHEN DEB-bie came out of Biology 201. She was juggling a sizable pile of books and laughing with friends when she spied him, and she immediately broke loose and pushed through the swarm of students.

"Hi, Daddy." She was worried.

"Hi, baby," he said. "Got a minute we can talk?"

"Sure. Is anything wrong?"

"No, no. Nobody is hurt or anything like that. I want to hear from you what went on when you drove out to the parish."

"Okay. You want to go sit outside?"

They found an empty bench beside the grassy quadrangle, shaded by a magnolia tree.

He asked her to start at the beginning, so she did. When she told about being turned away by the guard at the Bayou Disposal plant, he interrupted to ask if she had given her name. She said she hadn't, to Tubby's relief. She gave a blow-by-blow account of her meeting with the crawfishermen.

"What did the man say?" Tubby asked.

"It sounded like 'Bin Minny' to me, Daddy. Do you know what that means?"

"I think so," Tubby said. "He's a powerful man among those people. He was a colonel or something in the South Vietnamese army. He didn't come out with the first wave, but got caught and reeducated in some camp. It must not have taken hold because he jumped on a boat and somehow got to New Orleans. He's got a restaurant, and he's got a reputation, like some kind of Vietnamese mafioso. I don't know how much of it's true. I've never met him."

"Why would they mention him?" Debbie asked.

"It could be they think he can solve their problem better and faster than you and me."

"What can he do?"

"I have no idea."

"Then shouldn't we see what we can do to stop Bayou Disposal ourselves, right away?"

A delicate moment. Lawyering talent was called for.

"I've told Twink to write me a report about what happened, and I think you should, too. Your group knows better than I do how to get the attention of the EPA, and I'll be glad to call or write anybody you tell me to. If we can get any hard evidence, like even a signed statement, from one of the fishermen, we can try to get a restraining order against the company. I know you're a grown woman now, but this is developing into a very dangerous situation. There's some involvement here with Potter Aucoin, and he's dead. His man Broussard is dead. I'm going to have a particularly hard time concentrating on the legal aspects of this case if I'm worrying about you traipsing down to Plaquemines Parish interviewing people."

"You're asking me to quit now?"

He was screwing it up, but it wasn't over yet.

"No. Of course not. I need someone dedicated like you to help with all the legal research. But let someone else go out looking for affidavits."

Debbie looked at him searchingly for a minute, then she broke out laughing.

"Daddy, you're trying to protect me."

He opened his mouth, then shut it.

"You're damned right," he said.

"I think I'm too old for that," she said. "But I promise you I'll be careful. I'll talk over with the group who should do what. I won't go looking for trouble, that's all I can say." She patted his hand like he was a doddering old fool in a nursing home.

"Just look out for yourself," Tubby said, gracious in defeat. They hugged when they parted.

Resolving and closing the Bayou Disposal file was now the paramount concern in Tubby's life.

NICK THE NEWSMAN LEFT A MESSAGE THAT TUBBY should drop by.

"Watch the office for a while, will you please, Cherrylynn? I'll bring you back some lunch."

"I brought my Weight Watchers for the microwave, boss."

"Oh, well, I'll bring you back some dessert."

"Great," she laughed.

Nick was a little man. He sat on a high stool behind a counter in his newsstand. He carried papers and magazines from everywhere, and they overflowed racks on the walls, the floor, and all around him. He was hard to see when you walked in; his head looked just like another magazine cover stuck to the wall. Maybe a wrestling magazine.

There were a couple of men browsing the racing news when Tubby walked in, and a young woman with spiked orange hair studying something called *Sappho Sisterhood*. Tubby brushed past her and went to the counter.

Nick raised his eyebrows in welcome and scratched his chin whiskers.

"Here comes trouble," he said.

"Hiya, Nick. I got a message you called."

"Yeah." Nick beckoned him to come closer. Tubby bent over, and Nick put an arm around his shoulder. "You asked me who Charlie Van Dyne worked for," Nick whispered hoarsely, letting

Tubby get the full flavor of the onion rings Nick had stuck in the drawer of his cash register along with the remainder of his lunch.

"Right," Tubby said, gasping for air.

"Well, think about this. He had a legitimate job."

"So tell me while I can still breathe."

Nick grinned and tightened his hug. "He was a so-called rehabilitation counselor. He worked for Sheriff Mulé."

"No way."

"That's it. Check the record."

"I thought the sheriff was an honest dude."

"You ain't that big a fool," Nick exclaimed, dismayed.

"I guess it is suspicious when civil servants can afford to drive a Cadillac and live in a big house on Persephonie Street, isn't it?"

"Hey, go figure," Nick said. "It's the same thing with all dem democrats, am I right?" He bared all of his cigar-stained teeth for Tubby's pleasure.

"Uh, Nick . . ." Tubby began.

"You mind if I buy a newspaper?" a young woman trying to get in front of the register demanded.

"Let me tend to my customers, Tubby."

"Okay, Nick, see you." On the way out the door he asked himself what he was about to say to Nick, and what good it would have done.

Tubby's mind was in a whirl as he walked back toward Canal Street. He even passed the pie man sitting on the steps in front of the Wildlife and Fisheries Building, which is what people called the state Supreme Court, before he remembered Cherrylynn's dessert. Recovering, he walked back and got her a pecan pie, then thought maybe she would like a coconut better so he got her one of those, too. Intrigue always made him hungry, so he picked up a couple of sweet potatoes for himself for later. The old man put all four in a plastic bag, which Tubby placed carefully into his briefcase. Always a good idea to lay in provisions, he thought. It can be a long road between pie men.

BACK IN HIS OFFICE, TUBBY WANTED TO TALK TO TANIA to let her know about the connection with Sheriff Mulé, but more than anything else he just wanted to hear her voice. He thought she might not want him to call her at work, but he did it anyway.

A woman answered, "First Alluvial Bank," and put him through to Miss Thompson.

"Hi, it's me," he said.

"Oh, hello, Tubby. Is anything the matter?"

"No, I guess not. I just wanted to see if you had had any more trouble."

"Everything is fine," she said, picking her words carefully because she was on the job.

"No threats? No one following you?"

"Nothing obvious. Sometimes I think I see things."

"Do you see anything that looks like a police investigation?"

"No. My brother Thomas is getting out of the hospital tomorrow."

"How's his knee?"

"They say he'll walk good as new, but it's up to him if he ever plays sports again. It will just take lots of work, but he's determined to do it."

"If he wants to badly enough, I'm sure he will. Uh, I wanted you to know that Charlie Van Dyne had a job with the Sheriff's Department. He worked under Sheriff Mulé."

She was silent.

"I'm going to try to talk to the sheriff and get a read on the situation."

She still didn't say anything.

"I'm not going to tell him your name. I'll just be looking for information."

"Okay."

"Well, take care of yourself."

"I will."

"Call me if anything, you know, happens," he said.

She promised she would.

SHERIFF FRANK MULÉ AGREED TO SEE TUBBY AND TOLD him to come down to the jail—a small word for a big place. Actually, the sheriff had about five blocks of buildings under his control. The old-fashioned, barbed-wire-encased Parish Prison took up one block, as did Central Lockup, where everyone from vagrants to body slashers got processed. Then there was the diagnostic center, the windowless Community Correctional Center, some tent camps, and a variety of satellite institutions and former motels where extra prisoners were stashed. Most days Sheriff Mulé had more miserable outcasts and outlaws packed into his frightening cellblocks than the warden of the state prison farm at Angola had in his. Mulé kept them in line, too. The sheriff had a lot of people working for him who knew how to handle complaints.

Tubby only wanted to know about one of them, Charlie Van Dyne.

He took the elevator to Mulé's office and told the blonde secretary who he was.

"You've been here before," she commented. She looked sharp, in a stormtrooper kind of way.

"Yes." He smiled.

After a few minutes Mulé said he could come in.

The sheriff, all 120 pounds of him, sat behind a desk as big as a craps table. He was drawing a picture with crayons.

"What do you think?" he asked, holding it up for Tubby to see. It looked like a Tyrannosaurus rex tearing apart a big yellow cat.

"Powerful," Tubby said.

"I got a new program in mind," Mulé said. "Sit down, why don't you, counselor?" Tubby sat. "Instead of all that historical military stuff the last sheriff had the men painting, I've thought about having them draw animal life, like dinosaurs and elephants in the jungle."

"You mean like for murals on the side of buildings?" Tubby asked.

"Exactly. Keep the men busy, encourage the talents they have, but let them paint something they can relate to—the struggle for survival. The law of the jungle."

"You don't think maybe that's too bloody to put out where people on the streets can see it?"

"Sure, and war's not violent?" the sheriff asked sarcastically. "I'm thinking painting scenes from nature might put the men's minds onto life's important lessons."

"You could be right."

"Just a thought, I guess." The sheriff tossed the drawing onto the rug behind his desk.

"What can I do for you, Mr. Dubonnet? Last time you were here was about that drug pusher, Darryl what's-his-name. Then he got killed. Now what you want?"

"I'm trying to find out about a man named Charlie Van Dyne."

"Who's he?"

"He worked for you."

"So what. And he's dead, too. You got some perverse interest in people who get killed?"

"Well, I heard he was into selling drugs."

"Where'd you hear that?"

"It's just something I heard. A friend of mine is also involved somehow, and is getting death threats herself. I'm trying to find out what the truth is about Van Dyne and who he worked with to see if there's anything I can do to remove my friend from danger."

"You come in here saying one of my people was into selling drugs, which would make me look bad." The sheriff's voice rose. "You act like I know something about it, which is like accusing me of something. Just who the fuck do you think you are? You hit me with a habeas corpus petition on some twerp named Jerome Cook. Just what's the matter here? Now you're asking insulting questions about my employees. You trying to start something with me?" Mulé slammed his hand down on the desktop.

"I'm not accusing you of anything, Sheriff," Tubby said, taken aback. "I'm just looking for some information, and maybe some help."

"You ain't getting any help from me with something stupid like that. That ain't the way to get things done around here." The sheriff's dark face was red, and he looked like he was breaking a sweat.

"Look, this is a courtesy call. I'm trying to be cooperative with you."

"You won't get my cooperation like this," the sheriff fired back.

"I guess I'll be going then," Tubby said. The sheriff did not try to stop him so Tubby got up and walked out the door.

The Valkyrie receptionist smiled sympathetically when he went past her to the elevator.

"The sheriff must have forgotten to take his pill this morning," Tubby told her, and punched the elevator button.

Inside his office, Sheriff Mulé picked up his telephone and made a call.

CHAPTER

Thirty

CRUISING DOWN CARONDELET STREET, TUBBY SUD-
denly heard the sound New Orleans motorists fear the most—the
approaching trumpets and drums of the St. Augustine Marching One Hundred. Oh no! Here came the yellow barricades,
pulled across the street by the city's finest. Just two cars blocked
the way between him and the corner of Canal, but it was the difference between an efficient afternoon of work and being caught in
a parade.

Desperately, Tubby looked behind him, but cars were
stretched down the block. No hope of backing up. Long experience had taught him that there was nothing to do in this situation
but to lock the car and watch the parade. Since the top was down
on his Corvair convertible, and it was a real pain to put it up, he
couldn't stray too far.

As he looked up Canal Street, he was relieved to see that it was
a short parade, as if for a convention. The approaching vanguard
consisted of two very tall black men wearing dark suits and purple
fezzes, holding between them a blue silk banner as wide as the avenue which proclaimed that the International Society of Morticians and Embalmers was in town. They were followed closely by a
disorganized but happy throng of well-dressed folk sporting but-
tons the size of paper plates which read 103RD ANNUAL ENTOMB-
MENT, NEW ORLEANS, LOUISIANA. These were the dignitaries, no
doubt. They were followed smartly by a really jazzy halftime show

of high-stepping girls from P.G.T. Beauregard Middle School, their red-and-silver leotards sparkling, their boots flashing. They were full of spirit because right behind them were the blaring horns and booming drums of the fabled St. Augustine High School Marching Band.

This was a deluxe show for the middle of the afternoon, but Canal Street shoppers, jaded by a lifetime of carnival, passed obliviously along the sidewalk, only occasionally giving in to the temptation to hop up and yell, "Throw me something, Mister." Quite a few friends and family members of the morticians and embalmers, however, stood on the curbs cheering while the routine life of the city went on around them. A meter maid snuck around giving out parking tickets. A couple of white-haired businessmen wearing seersucker suits with cuffed pants haggled a point outside the Boston Club, raising their voices to be heard over the din.

Ten minutes and he would be out of here, Tubby predicted. His feet tapped to the extra-loud version of "Big Chief."

The first float loomed behind the band, and Tubby couldn't believe his luck. It was Monster Mudbug, or Adrian, who with Tubby's help had defeated many a traffic ticket for driving his huge float on the public streets.

Adrian's presentation was a great, rolling, faux stainless-steel crawfish boiler, and he was a giant crawfish. Not some inartful foam creation, like a football team might have for a mascot, but a shiny, hard, red crustacean, making him look all glossy and wet, gyrating to the funky get-down music blaring from his major sound system. Four pretty girls, dressed in very little, but with a seaweed-waitress motif, clung precariously to different spots on the pot and pitched beads, and even boiled crawfish, into the air, to the delight of the fans. The Monster Mudbug float was a crowd pleaser, and it carried its own jumping mass of parade-fanciers alongside.

Tubby was pushed back by the people. But Monster Mudbug

spotted him out of his plastic thorax and gave Tubby the kind of respect so many craved.

He pointed a big claw at Tubby and whacked one of the girls until she saw what he wanted. Then, while the float rolled relentlessly on, the Monster and his helpers deluged Tubby with beads, trinkets, and cups. Crawfish, both plastic and sort-of-edible, showered him and all those in his vicinity.

Tubby ducked his head while the people around him grabbed in the air. He made his move for the plastic cups bouncing along the sidewalk in between the jumping feet. They carried the Monster's picture. He could use these at home.

Prizes hidden under his coat, Tubby waved at the receding float, and Monster Mudbug beat his chest in farewell.

Before long, the barricades were pulled aside and life returned to normal. Tubby stowed his cups under the seat, draped a few beads over the rearview mirror, and continued on his way.

HE GOT BACK TO HIS OFFICE IN TIME TO GET A CALL from his daughter Debbie. She was excited and very angry. She had walked over to her apartment after class and found that Twink's Chevy Blazer had been completely busted up. Seems he had parked it in her driveway.

Its windows were smashed. Its tires slashed. Spray paint on the upholstery. All the engine wires were cut. Her own trash can had been dumped in the front seat.

How could that happen in broad daylight? This city was going crazy. The police hadn't even come to look at it. Was there anything he could do? Did he think it had anything to do with Bayou Disposal? If so, how would anyone know that the Blazer was parked at her house? No one knew where she lived.

"No, of course not," he lied. Or maybe it wasn't a lie. Maybe this was just random street crime.

But just to be sure, why didn't she go over and spend the night at her mother's, or, better yet, with him?

"What good would that do?" she demanded.

"It would make me feel better," he responded.

She said she would think about it.

"Damn it, Debbie. I want you to go someplace safe."

"I'm going to call Marcos and have him come over."

He sputtered into the phone, and the conversation ended inconclusively.

He was looking out the window at the rush-hour traffic, backed up bumper to bumper on the high-rise bridge, when Leo Caspar called.

"Whatcha messing with my friend Botaswati?" he began.

"I didn't know he was your friend," Tubby said. "It has to do with a pro bono case I agreed to take for a student group at Tulane."

"What's pro bono?"

"It means I don't get paid, like a charity."

"Oh, well, I don't think you're doing any good for society. He tells me some lawyer is annoying him, and I ask who it is. It's a big surprise to find out it's someone who works for me. Mr. Botaswati is a very respectable businessman. He doesn't do anything wrong."

"I don't know if he does or not. I've been trying to get some simple information about a company called Bayou Disposal. I didn't know you were involved with him at all."

"I'm not involved. And I don't think you should be either."

"So what are you telling me?"

"I'm not telling you anything. Just think about it."

"All right. I'll think about it."

"Good," Caspar said. He hung up.

Tubby immediately rang Jake LaBreau at home. He told Jake about the call and asked what was going on.

"Two weeks ago I had free time and no hassles," he told Jake. "Now I got a friend who's dead, another man gets murdered outside my office, and I'm getting threatening phone calls from some slick little greaser, pardon my French, who thinks he owns the city."

"Somebody got murdered outside your office?"

Tubby told him about Broussard.

"I don't know anything about that," Jake said, "but you probably should tread lightly."

"No joke," Tubby yelled. "And why is your boss, Leo Caspar, so concerned about a company called Bayou Disposal? Why is he telling me to quit asking questions about it?"

Jake didn't reply for a moment. Then he said, "There are some wheels turning here that I don't understand yet. I'm looking into things right now."

"What the hell are you talking about, Jake? Speak English!"

"I can't tell you any details yet, Tubby. Leo is, uh, a potentially dangerous guy. I'm just starting to realize how dangerous. I'd be careful, if I were you."

"Jake, this is nuts. Tell me something."

"I gotta go, Tubby. I don't have answers yet. Really," he added.

"Jake . . ." Tubby implored, exasperation mounting, but he was talking to a dead line.

He went back out to the street, needing to walk and think about things. There was a connection between Bayou Disposal and the trashing of Twink's car, he was certain. The spreading violence, Aucoin's death and now Broussard's, must be related, too, but he couldn't get a handle on what tied it all together. Now he was so worried about Debbie's safety that he couldn't concentrate.

On Canal Street there were still fragments of necklaces and a few doubloons left over from the parade. He stepped into a McDonald's, something he almost never did, but there was little chance he would be bothered by anyone he knew. He got a cup of coffee and sat down. There was a young couple behind him who looked harmless enough, but as if on cue the well-groomed male began delivering a loud monologue to his date.

"This guy's tied up to the chair. And they start playing . . . what's that song? An Eagles song, or maybe a Steve Miller song. The point is this guy stands around with a switchblade knife and begins cutting on another guy, cutting off his ear, cutting his face, fucking with him. And it's a very powerful scene, because of the popular music. It's in that genre—weird violence. It was very disturbing. You'd love it."

Tubby threw away his coffee and left. He let his feet carry him along. Why would Leo Caspar take an interest in a Pakistani T-shirt vendor or a waste disposal company? He was approaching the Casino Mall Grandé, sidestepping the line of limousines and hotel courtesy vans that were picking up and dropping off gamblers at the colossal front entrance, when he saw Leo himself come down the steps and open the back door of a long white Cadillac. Mindful of Jake's words of caution, Tubby was considering whether to intercept or to avoid the man when he saw Nicole run down the steps after him. Leo held the car door while she slipped in, then he got in and slammed it shut. The Cadillac pulled away and eased into the flow of Canal Street. Maybe there was nothing unusual about a boss and his assistant riding around in a limousine together, but it got him thinking.

He did not have the reasons for it, but he was convinced that Leo Caspar was behind Potter Aucoin's death. Some way or another, Caspar was responsible. More to the point, Caspar, or Botaswati, or someone in their ring, had threatened his daughter. He had always tried to keep the seamy side of his law practice away from his family, but now he was flunking the test and he didn't know why. He was spooked and could not suppress the illogical fear that this might be a punishment for his own misdeeds along the way. Distraught, and seeing conspiracies all around him, Tubby decided it was time to take matters into his own hands.

HE CALLED KATHY JEANSONNE AT THE *TIMES-PICAYUNE*.

"Are you still interested in the Potter Aucoin case?" he asked.

"Sure," she said. "It's one of many in my unsolved murders file, but I haven't forgotten about it yet."

"Well, I've got a tip for you."

"Shoot."

"There's a link between his death and a company called Bayou Disposal. It's run by some questionable characters." He told her a little bit about what the company was doing down in the marsh, and what the fishermen were saying.

"Can you document the connection?"

"No, but even if there's not one, just breaking the story about the dumping would be big news."

"Maybe. Who are the bad people running Bayou Disposal?"

"One just might be Leo Caspar, who manages the Casino Mall Grandé." This was, of course, pure conjecture.

"Really," she exclaimed. "Can you prove that?"

"No, but you might be able to. Why don't you ask the Vietnamese fishermen if they know Caspar. They may do some of your research for you."

Jeansonne was interested. She said that she might take a photographer down to Plaquemines Parish that very afternoon. Tubby told her where to go.

When she hung up he reflected on the possible consequences of his call. He told himself there was nothing unethical about using the press to advance a cause. Good and reputable lawyers did it all the time. Not everyone would agree, however, that this cause was noble.

Tubby didn't exactly think it was either. He wouldn't want to explain it in a court of law. Call it an eye for an eye, or call it protecting the home, take your choice. Someone had smashed up his daughter's friend's car in broad daylight. Who that message was intended for, Tubby wasn't absolutely positive, but now he was sending out a message of his own. How was this any different than what Tania had done? he asked himself. Not much, was the answer.

"Tough luck, dude," he said aloud to the empty room, sounding harder than he felt. He had a need to drink.

CHAPTER

Thirty-One

RED PEPPERS HUNG IN STRINGS FROM THE CEILING AND onions and green cabbages were heaped in white hampers against the wall. Three serene-faced young men steadily created colorful piles of chopped vegetables on a stainless-steel counter, while behind them the chef chattered excitedly to his assistants who were madly tending vast sizzling frying pans and steamy pots of noodles.

All stole a quick glance at the photographer and the red-haired lady who came into the kitchen with their boss, but they didn't break their pace. If anything, they sped up to look their best.

"This is where the magic happens," Bin Minny said proudly to Kathy Jeansonne, white teeth smiling under a mascara-line mustache. He spread out his small hands to take in the busy room.

"Shoot pictures if you like," he told the cameraman. "We're very proud of this kitchen, the cleanliness, the chef, the ingredients we use. We have taken the finest restaurant in Saigon and moved it here to New Orleans. Our fish is the best. Caught every day."

His oval eyes were too large for his head, Jeansonne thought. His trim body was too slight to account for the great deference shown him by everyone in the restaurant, employees and diners alike.

"Mr. Minh," she began, for she had learned that was his correct name, "do you have other businesses besides the Empress of Saigon?"

"None that so interest me," he said. "Would you like to taste one of the dishes?"

"Not right now." Jeansonne couldn't help but return Minh's persistent smile. "I have a deadline, and I really must ask you something."

"Certainly, ask whatever you like."

"I've talked to some Vietnamese fishermen down in Plaquemines Parish. They seem to respect you very much."

"Yes? That is good."

"Yes. They're having trouble with a company polluting their water supply. A company called Bayou Disposal."

Bin Minny stared at her blankly.

"They seem to believe that you are going to do something to help them."

"Perhaps they exaggerate my powers."

"Well, why would they think this? How would you help them?"

"That I cannot say."

"Do you know anything about Bayou Disposal? Do you know anything about a man named Leo Caspar?"

"No, who is he?"

"Mr. Caspar is the manager of Casino Mall Grandé. I have heard that he also runs Bayou Disposal."

Jeansonne, watching Bin Minny, had the strangest sensation that his eyes closed, but she was staring into them and they were quite open. His smile did not waver.

"I cannot satisfy your curiosity on this point," he said. "If you want to write about my restaurant, I would be honored, but the rest of this is just so many dreams and nightmares."

"Do you know Mr. Caspar?"

"The tour is over," Bin Minny said.

He signaled to the men slicing vegetables, who instantly stopped their frantic activity and stepped into the aisle to face the reporter and her photographer.

Without another word, Bin Minny passed through them and exited the kitchen at the rear.

"I don't want to order anything," the photographer said, looking around at the figures in the suddenly quiet kitchen.

The news team backed out the swinging doors and retreated from the scene.

CHAPTER Thirty-Two

TUBBY TRIED TO REACH LEO CASPAR IN THE MORNING. He had thought about it and decided that Caspar knew the way through the maze, and he was seized with a compulsion to tie the man down and interrogate him. Or, more in line with his personal nature, to negotiate with him.

But the secretary said Mr. Caspar was too busy to talk to him. When he called again an hour later it was the same thing, and an hour after that.

In the meantime Tubby tried to concentrate on Bubba Pender's contract to transfer his rights to his miracle potato peeler to Magnabuks, the international dicer and slicer conglomerate, but without much luck. He ordered up a Ferdi from Mother's to take his mind off things, but even thick slices of turkey, blackened ham, roast beef, and hot debris gravy on French, though momentarily and monumentally gratifying, couldn't make him stop thinking about Caspar and how he kept appearing at the center of things.

He tried a third time and got the same message, so he told Cherrylynn to hold the fort and set off walking to the casino. His face was recognized, and he was admitted to the office area, but Leo was not around. He found Nicole sitting at her desk. She said she didn't know where Leo was, but once more she invited Tubby out for a cup of coffee.

"Sure," he said, concealing his impatience, "but not here."

She got her purse and they squeezed through the garment workers to the traffic-flavored air outside. Good coffee had never been hard to find in New Orleans, but nowadays it was hard to miss. Coffeehouses were popular again, and a new one had just opened up on Natchez Street near the casino. At the counter Tubby asked if they had any coffee with chicory and was told that chicory was a special flavor available only on Tuesdays. Just a bit annoyed, he ordered what the chalkboard described as Colombian Java. From the ceiling a foreign-accented PBS commentator relayed the latest news from eastern Europe.

"Tubby, you seem distracted," Nicole observed.

"I was wondering who makes all the different coffee beans. I mean, do they flavor them down in Colombia, or is it something they just spray on in a back room here?"

"I have no idea."

"Seems to me with this many coffeehouses popping up, we need to find out. Have you worked for Caspar long?"

"A year or two."

"What kind of man is he?"

"What do you mean?"

"Is he the kind of boss who lets you alone, or does he tell you what to do?"

"Mr. Caspar takes an interest in everybody who works for him. He's been very generous with me."

"Generous?"

"I'm well paid for what I do. There's nothing wrong with that, is there?"

"No."

"It's the same with you, isn't it, Tubby?"

"Well paid? I try to be."

"Do you think you're also fighting for some kind of justice?"

"As a lawyer?" Tubby laughed. "Well, maybe I do," he said.

"I thought you probably did."

Tubby did not want to like Nicole just then.

"I've been trying to see your boss," he said. "Is there anything you can do to arrange a meeting?"

"I don't know. Leo has been real busy. If it's important, I could see what I can do."

"It's important to me. You can tell him it has to do with Potter Aucoin."

"Who's that?" she asked innocently.

"A guy who got killed," Tubby said, watching her carefully. He didn't see any reaction.

"If you say so," she replied uncertainly.

An hour after they parted she called him at the office.

"Leo asked me to tell you he would be tied up all day in meetings. He'll be in the French Quarter tonight, and he can meet you at a bar called The Hard Rider at eight o'clock. He invited me to come, too." Why wasn't Tubby surprised that The Hard Rider was the conference room of choice?

"Whatever you say, Nicole."

"You don't sound too enthusiastic about me being there."

"I'm sorry. They say you should never mix business with pleasure."

"You men can talk business, then we can turn our attention to pleasure."

Tubby told her he would be at Botaswati's bar at eight o'clock. He didn't expect to get much enjoyment out of it.

CHAPTER

Thirty-Three

NIGHTTIME BROUGHT A LIVELY SCENE TO THE HARD Rider. The bar was packed two deep with noisy men. Old disco dance hits pounded off the ceiling. Lots of flashy neon advertising beer and spring water festooned the walls. There were other men wearing jackets and ties like Tubby, as if they had just come from work. One thing about New Orleans, there was hardly anyplace you looked funny dressed up. There was also hardly anyplace that would kick you out for wearing clean shorts and sneakers. The Hard Rider welcomed both kinds. Both kinds nodded at Tubby when he came in.

Not all the customers wore pants. Beauties of uncertain gender were the center of attention at a corner table. And Nicole suddenly appeared at his side.

"Hey, mister, would you like to dance?"

"It's not my kind of music."

"We could make our own."

"At least I wouldn't have to do an anatomy check to see what I was dancing with."

"I suppose not," she said, and he thought she blushed.

"Where's Leo?"

"He's upstairs. Follow me."

There were stairs at the back of the bar, blocked by a locked gate. Nicole waved at the bartender, the same Vietnamese woman who had been there when Tubby first visited. She pressed a button somewhere that made the lock pop open with a thunk.

The stairs were narrow and dimly lit, but Nicole led the way with assurance. At the top, a long hallway ran the length of the building, with closed doors along it. Tubby walked behind Nicole to the end, where she knocked at the last door.

It opened, and Nicole stood aside to let Tubby pass. It was a nervous Botaswati who held the door for him. Mr. Caspar was lounging comfortably in his business suit on a couch against the far wall. There were two other men, both large size, in the room, standing like bookends at either side of the couch. They gave the impression of being former athletes. Both wore Docksiders, Duck Head pants, and baggy cotton sports shirts.

"Good evening," Botaswati said, and to Caspar, "I will be downstairs." Caspar winked an eyeball, and Botaswati slipped out and closed the door behind him.

Nicole smiled at Tubby and started to leave, too, but Caspar stopped her.

"Stay with us, sis," he said. "Come sit with me."

She looked like the idea didn't strike her fancy, but she went to the couch and sat as directed, demurely crossing her legs. They became the focal point of those assembled until Caspar spoke.

"You wanted to see me, Mr. Dubonnet?"

"Yep," Tubby said. "Privately."

"This is a private meeting. Sit." He indicated a red plastic chair leaning against the wall. One of the beefy boys righted it with his foot and slid it forward. Tubby put it in the center of the room and sat facing Caspar.

"Now, what did you want to talk to me about?" Caspar said, as if he were truly curious.

"I think you've got an interest in some companies, like Bayou Disposal and Ship Ahoy, too. Maybe you own them, maybe not. You've got Bijan Botaswati fronting for you. Bayou Disposal was dumping chemicals into the river and probably onto the ground.

That's against the law. You could get substantial fines to cover clean-up costs."

"So what's it to you?"

"The dead man, Potter Aucoin, the one who saw it happen, that's what it is to me."

Caspar looked like he was thinking it over.

"I don't understand it," he said. "Nobody cares about what kinda crap may be spilled on the levee. Christ, it's all over town. Toxic waste. Environmental hazards. I don't care about that stuff, and nobody else does either. You seem to have a nose for unprofitable lines of thought."

"Maybe, but I'm not stinking up the world either. Now your outfit is down in Plaquemines Parish fouling up the fishing down there."

"Don't you like the work you're doing for us? I thought you were a reasonably intelligent man, not some save-the-whales nut. You and Reggie Turntide have a reputation for knowing how to solve problems. Not create them."

"Reggie is no longer my partner. And you don't have to be a nut to like to catch fish."

"Whatever. We hired you. We expect a little loyalty and discretion. Here, calm down. Play another game with me." He pulled a deck of cards out of his coat pocket and handed it to Nicole, who looked at it as if she had no idea what it was used for.

"Offer the cards to Mr. Dubonnet," Caspar explained. "Let him cut."

She held out her hand with the deck in her palm. Tubby stared into her eyes, which looked worried, and cut light. He turned up a three of clubs.

Caspar shook his head.

"Are you trying to be a loser?" he asked without humor as he studied the deck. Then he reached over quickly and slid a card out with his pinkie finger and thumb. It was a two of hearts.

"You see," he said. "You can be a winner. But you gotta stick with me." He tossed a William McKinley at Tubby. "That was for five hundred bucks," he said. "Now what else we got to meet about?"

"The main thing is," Tubby said, looking at the strange bill, "my friend. Somebody has to answer for that."

"You have a jumble of facts in your mind, Mr. Dubonnet, but you don't know how to put them together. I don't give a flying fuck about river pollution. I've tried to make that clear."

"I'm just looking for answers, Leo. Who killed Aucoin?"

"That I can't help you with."

"Oh well." Tubby looked at the money for the last time. "I guess the reason you can't help me is because you are the one who had him killed. And I also think you had his foreman, Broussard, shot in my building."

"Now you've crossed the line, Mr. Dubonnet." Caspar shook his head sadly. "It might surprise you to know," he added, "that I did not even know that your friend had made such an allegation until you told me."

"Then why did he die?" Tubby demanded.

"All I can tell you is your friend was stubborn and blind to his own self-interest. Much like yourself. I told you it would not be smart for you to continue your investigation of this matter."

"It's not something I have a choice about, believe me."

"Too bad. You should have listened to me. But if I leave you alone you're going to continue to probe. You're going to continue to send people out to my operations, stirring up the neighbors."

"I didn't actually send them," Tubby said.

"But they went. One of them was, I think, a relation of yours. Your daughter?"

Tubby didn't say anything. He looked at Nicole, but she was studying her own fingers twisting around in her lap.

"You're a pain in the butt, Mr. Dubonnet. You won't go with the program. That gives me no choice but to remove you."

This bad news gave Tubby an adrenaline rush. The word ESCAPE flashed in bright neon before his eyes. He knocked over his chair and jumped for the door, but the two muscle men were also in motion. One had a hand on him before he could turn the knob. He punched backward with his elbows and swung wildly with his free hand, but both men were quickly upon him, crushing him against the wall. He started to yell but by then he was facedown on the floor, and the yell was more of an agonized grunt.

A knee crunched into his kidneys, taking his breath away in a rush of pain. His arms were bent roughly behind his back. He struggled unsuccessfully as a handkerchief was pulled into his mouth and yanked tight until his cheeks felt like they were pinned to his ears. His wrists were taped together. Through bulging eyes he could see Nicole, her legs still primly crossed, and her hands up at her lips as if to say, Oh, my, my.

And Tubby could also see Leo the Weasel, sitting calmly but attentively, watching as his bidding was done. He laid his hand on Nicole's knee. She stared at it for a moment, and then clutched it tightly in both of her own. But suddenly Caspar's eyes opened wide in surprise, and he scrambled to his feet.

The door behind Tubby had banged open. The knees left Tubby's back as Francis and Courtney arose to engage a more proficient enemy. Tubby rolled onto his back, trying to get out of the way and trying to see what was going on. He had to keep twisting to avoid being hit by falling bodies. Francis and Courtney were on the floor, suffering from unknown injuries and not moving.

Tubby's scrambled brain perceived three Vietnamese men incorrectly dressed in checkered sports jackets and loose slacks, bearing wooden sticks and handguns, stepping over the bodies on the floor and surrounding the startled Caspar. One stuck something in Caspar's mouth to keep him quiet, and another stuck something in his arm. Leo went limp. Nicole, on the other hand, came suddenly alive and broke for the door like a deer from cover. One of the men stabbed out with his wooden stick and caught her on the bridge of her nose with an audible thwack. It stopped Nicole in mid spring, and without further comment she pitched to the floor, joining the heap.

Tubby tried on his let's-all-be-friends smile, but his gag didn't give him much cheek to work with. It didn't matter because the urban guerrillas weren't paying any attention to him. They swiftly buried their weapons in their clothes, straightened each other's lapels, and, supporting Leo like a drunken comrade, dragged him from the room and were gone.

Tubby rolled around some more, but the view didn't change. Three bodies down and him hog-tied. Then he remembered he could sit up. After more gyrating than he would have wanted any-body to see, he got his wrists to one of the overturned chairs and began rubbing his bindings up and down against the edge of the seat. Finally the fabric parted, and his hands came free. He tore off his gag.

He checked Nicole first. She was blowing gentle blood bub-bles out of her nose, so she was definitely alive. One of the athletes had a heartbeat, but he wasn't sure about the other one. He picked up Nicole and laid her on the couch, where she appeared to be a little more comfortable, though still not her best. They say you lie down with dogs, you wake up with fleas. Tubby left the room.

He walked down the hall quietly, conscious of a major pain in his lower back where something important might have popped loose, and he limped cautiously down the stairs. The gate at the bottom could be unlatched from the inside, and he pulled it aside to step into the barroom. The crowd was still there, rocking and rolling. Unsteadily, he forced his way toward the front. He locked eyes with the lady behind the bar, who watched his passage without showing any expression he could read. He pushed open the ornate door and got outside to the street. It was much quieter out here.

Tubby leaned against the brick building and got his bearings. A man carrying a bag of groceries from the A&P passed on the sidewalk and looked the other way. People here valued privacy.

Tubby lurched away toward Canal Street. He would try to find a cab there and get the hell home.

CHAPTER
Thirty-Four

TUBBY STAYED INDOORS THE NEXT MORNING AND nursed his wounds. He called Cherrylynn to say he was feeling ill, which he was. She said he had no messages. By midmorning, however, he was overcome by curiosity, and he called Jake LaBreau. Coyly, he asked Jake again if Jake knew why Caspar had told Tubby to stay away from Bayou Disposal.

Jake said he didn't want to talk on the phone. He asked if Tubby could meet him for a drink a little later at Le Meridian. Tubby said fine. He conducted so much of his business in bars and restaurants he wondered why he even kept an office.

He scanned his front yard carefully through a slit in the curtains before he eased out the door to his car.

They settled down with midday martinis and a big bowl of macadamias and Brazil nuts at a candlelit table away from the piano. It was way too early for a crowd, and one of the few other customers was idly tinkering with "St. James Infirmary" on the Yamaha keyboard. Jake looked worried and tired, much as Tubby did.

"He's pretty good," Tubby said, making conversation.

"Yeah. I wish I had some talent," Jake said. "Then I could quit playing this game."

"I thought you liked public relations," Tubby said. Apparently Jake hadn't heard anything about the events of last night. Tubby did not enlighten him.

"I do occasionally. It fits my personality. It's all such a joke, though. Don't you think so?"

"Public relations?"

"All this stuff." Jake's sweeping gesture enclosed the known universe. "Some kid will shoot you on the street just to see what's in your wallet. You can get AIDS from a blow job. Don't you think it's a joke?"

"Ha. Ha. Are we feeling a little cynical today?" Tubby certainly was.

"What, a cynical ad man? I went to an interesting party this week."

Tubby nodded to show he was keeping up. He fished for his olive with the plastic sword.

"You know who Joe Caponata is?"

"I've heard of him." Mr. Caponata used to be called the mafia don, if there was such a thing, of New Orleans. He was semiretired.

"I got invited to a wine and cheese at the lovely Caponata home a couple of days ago. Very nice. Mr. Caspar took me. In fact, Mr. Caspar told me I ought to go."

"And what happened?" Tubby prodded.

"Not a lot. Leo paid his respects. It seems he is kind of the adopted son of Mr. Caponata."

"What do you mean, adopted son?"

"Actually, I don't think he really is adopted. Not legally. But Caspar calls him Poppa Joe. And Joe seems to be very fond of Leo. They hug. They talk. Old Mr. Joe puts his arm around Leo."

"Leo wanted you to see this?"

"Evidently so, kiddo. Leo is letting me take a peek at what his hole cards are."

"You think this is something the State Gaming Commission might like to hear about?"

"It's not exactly part of my job description to communicate bad publicity to the commission, Tubby. To tell you the truth, I'm thinking about me right now. I'm looking around for a new job, but I've got to be kind of, uh, careful about how I go about it. I don't want anybody to be, you know, worried about me, you know what I mean?"

"Yes," Tubby said.

"So, old buddy, this conversation is real confidential, okay?"

"Sure."

"Now it's show-and-tell time. What has Leo asked you to do for us?"

"Look at your alcohol permits for the sidewalk café. Nothing very controversial in that, is there?"

Jake looked puzzled.

"No, I can't see anything odd in that, except I thought we had permits out the kazoo."

"It sure looks that way to me."

"The thing that seems strangest about it, though, is that it was Mr. Caspar who told me to use you as a lawyer."

That was a surprise.

"Don't get me wrong," Jake said. "It seemed like a good idea to me. I've known you for a long time, Tubby, but it's not my position to decide what law firm to use, so nobody asked my opinion. And I don't know why Leo wanted you."

"Neither do I," Tubby said.

"I bring it up because I'm trying to get the lay of the land here."

"You've got me real curious, too."

"There's another thing. Maybe I ought not to tell you this, but I really think you should know."

"So what is it?" Tubby asked.

"It's what I needed to check out when we talked yesterday. This is also confidential. The company wants to float a riverboat.

They're looking at several locations to build the dock. All hush-hush, of course."

"They want to get the property before word gets out and prices skyrocket, right?"

"Exactly. But I'm going to tell you because you're our lawyer. One possible spot is St. Ann Street."

"Good location. Right in the French Quarter."

"Sure, but that area on the river is subject to about sixteen different leases that will take at least two centuries or an unbelievable amount of payoffs to unwind. And it's in the domain of the Vieux Carré Commission—not exactly the gambler's friend. The second is the Tuscany Street wharf."

"Up by the ferry landing?"

"Way past, but that's right. Better politics—the main thing you got to deal with is the Levee Board, and they're in the bag—but it's incredibly dangerous. It's like a magnet. Ships hit that wharf all the time. The Corps of Engineers have even studied it to figure out why. It's some freak thing with the current. Imagine the work for lawyers when an oil tanker spears a convention full of three thousand gambling orthopedic surgeons and dumps them all into the river."

"Yes, indeed," Tubby said, and smiled.

"So, Mr. Caspar explains to me after the party is over, he thinks the company should reject those two. There's a third site he wants me to help him promote. It's one that some local investors have an interest in—like Joe Caponata, like Sheriff Mulé. You get the picture?"

"Not yet, but that's a mighty bad combination."

"Now you're seeing the joke. This is the little secret Leo is letting me in on. If the company picks the third site, I'll make out like a bandit. If we don't, I'll be in the shitter."

"Who makes the decision?"

"Ultimately? The board of directors in New York. But they don't know beignets from bagels. They just read consulting reports, and we hire the consultants. I'm surprised Mr. Caspar hasn't hired you, for example."

"Well, he hasn't. What's the third site?"

"It's at the end of Napoleon Avenue, right near the big wharf. It's got great parking, and the leases are under control."

Tubby put his drink down and leaned over the table. The picture was becoming clearer. "Where exactly on the riverfront is this, Jake?"

"I got a map. You want to see it?"

"Oh yes," Tubby said.

Jake took his briefcase from the chair beside him and unsnapped it. He extracted a file and a map, which he unfolded on the tabletop so that Tubby could look.

The area was the Napoleon Avenue wharf. As best as he could tell, the "Big Easy Promenade," as the boat dock was called on the schematic, was right about where the Export Products shed was now located, and the "Acres of Free Parking" were what used to be the Bayou Disposal truck yard.

"I noticed the curious connection when you mentioned Bayou Disposal to me," Jake said.

"Why is Leo involved with Bayou Disposal?"

"I don't know. But I'd say if he is, Joe Caponata is, too."

"Look, I'll see you, Jake. Be careful."

"I'm the most careful man alive. Next to you, of course."

"Right," Tubby said.

IT WAS ALMOST LIKE A MIST, THE WAY THE WORLD looked through Leo Caspar's eyes. Coming through the mist were brown faces with square jaws and dark creases for eyes. They drifted in and out, and he had the sensation of being carried and dropped, more than once, but without pain.

One face stood out. The nose was almost flat. The mouth was

very small and the lips were cracked, guarding a little city of rotten and jagged teeth. But Caspar felt no fear. Even when the man stepped back and showed Caspar a hand without fingers, and he recognized it as his own. Even when the man held up an arm and tossed it off to one side, out of the picture. Leo only experienced a twinge of sadness at losing it, but the man was showing him a foot now, and Leo started to feel a little regret.

DAWN WAS JUST BREAKING. THE CLOUDS IN THE EAST were glowing a faint pink, and a blue heron stood silently, one-legged, in the shallow pond. The peacefulness of the scene was en-hanced by the two fishermen near the far bank quietly baiting their traps. The putt-putt of the trawling motor on their flat-bottomed boat could barely be heard. A smoky mist was rising off the water. The men didn't speak. With stubs of burning cigarettes stuck in their chapped lips, they carefully went about their work—which was taking the raw chunks of meat and bone, cut up neatly by a band saw, out of a broken ice chest and putting the pieces, one at a time, into the crawfish traps.

Some of the pieces were juicy. Others looked oddly like frag-ments of a skull and had hardly any meat on them at all. The men worked slowly down one row and back up the next. Then the ice chest was empty, except for a gory slime on the bottom that would wash away with a hose, and they puttered off toward the dock. The sun was just breaking the horizon. Happy, happy crawfish.

NICK NICARRO, THE NEWSMAN, CALLED TUBBY AND SAID he wanted to see him right away. Tubby couldn't remember Nick ever saying that. Trying to keep his paranoia in check he took him-self to the French Quarter and stood in front of Nick's Royal Street shop.

Nick waved him in and climbed off his stool behind the counter. He motioned Tubby to follow him back to the corner where all the porno magazines were displayed in plastic wrap so the two could have a private talk, though the only other person in the store was a black gentleman wearing a blue pin-striped suit who was reading the day's *Racing Form.*

"You been in some kind of trouble, or what?" Nick demanded in a hoarse whisper.

"What do you mean?" Tubby whispered back.

"There are some guys asking about you. Word's out you're gonna get hurt."

"What guys?"

"Fuck if I know. I didn't see 'em. Mob guys."

Tubby looked worried. He was worried.

"You've helped me out of some jams, Tubby, is why I called you. Did you do something to cross Sheriff Mulé?"

"Huh?"

"First you ask me about this guy Charlie Van Dyne, who was the sheriff's boy until he got bumped off. Now people are asking about you."

"I thought you said the mob, like Joe Caponata."

"In my book, Tubby, Frank Mulé and Joe Caponata are like this." He clenched his fists together and shook them in front of Tubby's nose. "You gotta watch 'em both. They're snakes."

"What should I do, Nick?"

The Newsman's red-and-green eyes widened in distress. "You're the lawyer," he said, as if that meant powerful medicine. "Man, if you don't have some bright idea, you'd better leave town."

"Okay, well, thanks for the tip, Nick."

"Yeah, see you," Nick whispered, and it seemed like he was now anxious for Tubby to leave the store.

On the sidewalk outside, Tubby's fair city seemed scary, just like the Newsman always said it was.

CHAPTER Thirty-Five

TUBBY RETIRED TO MAKE A PLAN. HE STAYED AT HOME for two more days and tried to keep from jumping every time a car passed or a tree limb tapped against the window while he considered the problem. His best move was that he talked Debbie into attending a conference on wilderness preservation in Austin and gave her his credit card number to pay for the trip. Marcos was traveling with her. Tubby studied the newspapers, but there was nothing in them about the events at The Hard Rider. That didn't mean the wheels weren't turning. He was afraid for his life. He was afraid for Debbie's safety. Sitting around was giving him chest pains.

On Wednesday morning he cut himself shaving, and his frustration got the better of him. He threw his razor down and forced his mind to engage. It boiled down to two choices. With Leo missing, either he could confront the arrogant, bristling sheriff who had already kicked him out of his office, or he could try to make peace with the evil mafia boss whom he knew only from the newspapers. The idea of calling Detective Kronke and placing the whole mess in the hands of the police crossed his mind fleetingly, but, he asked himself, what cop was going to lay a hand on Mulé? They don't have the push, he told the face in the mirror. Squaring his jaw and summoning an angry glare to reassure himself, he chose Caponata.

Mr. Mike said he knew where Caponata lived, but he asked questions that Tubby didn't want to answer. He possibly could have set up a meeting, but it would have looked all wrong. Caponata would think he was doing a big favor, and he would remember Mike for all the wrong things when he heard what Tubby had to say. Tubby didn't want to tarnish Mr. Mike's golden years with a pissed-off Joe Caponata.

So he called Jake again. His friend's voice on the phone had a quiver to it that was new. The ad man's glowing hello was missing a few kilowatts.

The sands were shifting rapidly, Jake said. The hounds were after fresh meat, know what I mean? The butt slicer was working overtime.

"Heard anything from Mr. Caspar?" Tubby asked innocently.

"Not a peepster. He's gone, slick as grease, sight unseen, transferred out west, they say. No farewell party, his desk is cleaned out, new man's coming in tomorrow. It's party time here, Tub."

"And Nicole?"

"Nicole had a car accident, busted her nose, slight concussion, her face is all blue. She'll be out awhile. And me, Tubby, ol' Jake is doing fine. It's the white-knuckle express at the old casino."

"Sorry to hear that, Jake."

"Maybe I shouldn't have brought you into my happy family, Tubby. Nobody's been too happy lately."

"Not to worry. I would have had to meet the family anyway, sometime."

"Well, if anything strange should happen to me, I give you my pool, my wife, my mortgage, and my kids. You'll take care of them, won't you? See that the kids finish Jesuit? You can call them all Dubonnets."

"I'll try to make Beth a good husband. Look, Jake, have you got a phone number for Joe Caponata?"

"Jesus, Tubby, you're the suicidal one, aren't you? When did I meet you? Can we pretend we don't know each other?"

"Hey, man. Stress is fun, remember? That's what you used to tell me. You got a number?"

He did. And Tubby called it. Caponata wouldn't come to the phone, but after Tubby uttered some fairly direct passwords to the woman who answered, the old man invited Tubby to drop by the house that afternoon, say three o'clock.

THE NEIGHBORHOOD WAS NOT GRAND; IT WAS NICE. BIG stucco-and-brick homes, backing up to the lake. Nice sidewalks, nice lawns, clean-cut kids cruising around in expensive Nissans, private security parked on every other tree-shaded corner. Tubby had had it as the lone wolf, and for this interview he brought backup with him, in the person of Cherrylynn. Her job was to watch the Spyder and let someone know if Tubby never returned. She had brought magazines. He guessed she was also well armed with Mace, the working girl's friend. Cherrylynn believed in protection.

She stayed with the car, parked by the curb. He went to the big front door and clanked the knocker. A gray-haired woman let him in and told him to follow her. Moving slowly, she led the way down the Mexican-tiled hall, past attractively framed paintings, some of which Tubby recognized as the expensive work of local artists. He knew two of them.

He was shown into a spacious airy room at the rear of the house, with French doors opening onto a garden courtyard. Mr. Caponata was sitting in a wrought-iron chair at a round glass table. His face was an older version of the familiar one that had been in the newspapers over the years. A high brick wall, giving the appearance of great age, provided the patio with privacy. Epiphytic bromeliads, blushing and otherwise, and orchids living off the sultry air, were hung from old black nails driven into the mortar. Caponata was drinking a cup of coffee and reading the sports section.

He didn't get up when Tubby stepped outside, but he politely put down his paper and pointed to a chair at the table. Tubby sat.

"Coffee, Mr. Dubonnet?"

Tubby said yes.

Caponata carefully poured a cup from a white china pot on the table. He pushed it slowly across the glass, then, by raising his eyebrows, offered cream and sugar from a silver set.

Tubby shook his head.

Caponata sighed. "Why are you here, Mr. Dubonnet?" He looked weary.

"I want to work things out with you."

"What things, please? This is a time of sadness for me. I don't need a lot of small talk."

"I haven't got much patience for small talk either, Mr. Caponata." Tubby tried out his glare and plunged ahead. "People working for you killed a friend of mine. I'm pretty sure of that. You may or may not have known about it. His name was Potter Aucoin. He had a company down by the river, Export Products. Ever heard of it?"

Mr. Caponata didn't respond. He merely stared at Tubby.

Tubby coughed, rubbed his jaw, and then continued.

"It troubled me. Why did he die? I thought I knew, but now I'm not sure. I know who ordered it. Leo Caspar. Have you heard from Caspar?"

Caponata looked wounded. He bowed his head, and a tear worked its way down his nose. Tubby was disconcerted.

"Leo is dead," Caponata whispered.

Tubby relaxed.

"You know how it happened, I suppose?"

"Not yet, but I know the circumstances of his disappearance and that you were there." He looked up, and there was a blaze of anger in his eyes. Tubby saw what the man must have looked like when he was young.

"You bet I was there, tied up and ready to be tossed in the river. You know that, too?"

Caponata shrugged. "You're still around, aren't you? Leo's the one gone."

"You're mourning him?"

"Yes, but my grief is a private thing. It doesn't concern you."

"It concerns me very much. I'm entitled to see some suffering. I want to know that Potter Aucoin is a little bit paid for. I don't expect justice. I don't have much expectation that I could ever pin his death on you. I could try, of course," Tubby suggested hopefully.

"You're foolish if you think you could ever connect me with that, 'cause I never heard about it until you told me just now." Mr. Caponata patted his lips, then raised his eyes to Tubby's. They were gray, like Leo's.

"I doubt that's true," Tubby said, "but you may be right about connecting you to the murder. I'm sure you've covered your tracks well. Look, I'm no policeman. I'm not even a hard-assed lawyer. But I would like to understand why Potter died. There are reasons I have to stay with this until I find out." Tubby sounded almost apologetic.

"I'm sure you have your theories," Caponata murmured. "Everybody does about me."

"You're right. I do. One of them is that you never cared about any river dumping, or anything Potter saw. You just wanted his property. You wanted his lease. Am I right?"

Caponata did not reply. He just stared with distaste at Tubby.

"I just need to know," Tubby continued. "I'm not wired or anything like that."

"I'm not worried about your being wired, Mr. Dubonnet," Caponata chuckled. He gestured in the direction of the roof, where it extended over the patio. There was something round and electronic mounted there that Tubby would have taken for a small satellite dish for TV, if he had noticed it at all.

"I'll tell you one thing, Mr. Dubonnet," Caponata said after a pause. "It was at my suggestion that you were retained by Casino Mall Grandé. I was curious why a lawyer with a reputation as a loner, a man who keeps his head down, would want to be interested in the death of a nobody working down by the docks. I thought it would be a good idea to explore your motives a little bit. Maybe you were just trying to drum up a little business for yourself. That's okay. I understand lawyers who do that. Maybe you were trying to get into my real estate deal. That's not so okay. When I learned that you were giving my friend Botaswati a hard time, I said, yeah, he's trying to crash into my deal. But I tell Caspar, there's plenty here for everybody. Lawyers are sometimes good to have around. Invite Mr. Dubonnet to the party. Show him how sweet the gambler's life can be."

"It was real sweet for me. But not for Potter. That's the problem. He was my friend." Tubby shrugged. "As I see it, you want the casino to tie its riverboat up right where Export Products is located, and you want to put a parking lot right where Bayou Disposal's yard used to be. You had the parking lot lease all sewed up. Only Potter wouldn't vacate like a good boy. He wouldn't give you his lease, would he?"

"No, he wouldn't," Caponata said. "He was extremely uncooperative. It seemed no price would satisfy him."

"That doesn't sound like Potter."

"Well, no reasonable price would satisfy him. Your friend was a difficult man. He threatened, not to me, of course, but he threatened to report the discharge of chemicals, or whatever he claimed to have seen, to some kind of government outfit. But not out of any love for the fishies, Mr. Dubonnet. It was just a bargaining chip for him. If we had raised our offer enough, he would have withdrawn any statement he made. Do you doubt that?"

Tubby didn't really doubt that, though he liked to think well of the dead. Potter had been a good buddy, but Tubby had always thought the last bandwagon Potter would have jumped on would have been a campaign to get lots of government inspectors nosing around the docks.

"Then what was the problem?" Tubby asked.

"I'll tell you, and then I'll tell you why I'm telling you. Your friend screwed up. But, hey, I screwed up, too. We had this nice lease, on this nice land, right by the river. A good parking lot, lots of access. We'll plant trees, landscape it. Fantastic place for a gambling boat. Great location. We can sell this idea to the casino board of directors. But naturally we want to keep this quiet till all the pieces fall into place, so we look for a company to put on the land, just to hold it. Could have been any company. I got a lot of companies. But Leo picks the disposal company. Sounds okay, just a truck parking lot, really. And Leo was going to see that everything ran smooth. But these lazy asshole truck drivers were just pouring the crap right out on the ground. They probably poured it into the river when they got worried about walking around in all the puddles of muck they were making. That's the sad truth. But your friend got way out of line. He thought he could just nudge us a little, but he put his fucking finger right up my ass. That's when Leo maybe tried to put on some pressure of his own. What happened after that I can't say. I have no idea how your man Potter died. It wasn't intentional."

"No offense, Mr. Caponata, but that's bullshit. You know how he died and who did it. I might be able to put you in jail for this."

"I sincerely doubt that."

"Bijan Botaswati can tie you to Bayou Disposal."

"You will find that Mr. Botaswati, who I never heard of, has gone for an extended trip to Pakistan. He will be difficult to locate. But why would you want to put me in jail anyway, Mr. Dubonnet? I'm as sad about this as you are."

"For much different reasons."

"You think so? What do you think I'm made of? Marble? You don't think I cry when people get hurt?"

"That's not your reputation."

"And what do you say my reputation is?"

"That you were the mafia don of New Orleans. That you ran all the rackets here."

"I never could understand why people thought that. You want some more coffee?"

"No, thanks," Tubby said.

"How long have you lived in New Orleans, Mr. Dubonnet?"

"I came here for college and stayed."

"So, a long time. You see any big rackets? You see people walking around in fear of the mob? Of course not. This is a very easygoing place. The only racket we got around here is politics. And you ain't never seen no Caponata run for office."

"I imagine you've got your finger in quite a few pies."

"I've done okay, but I ain't no don. I'm admitting that to you. Sometimes it helped that people thought I was, I won't deny. But look—who's the don now, since I retired?"

Tubby thought about it.

"I don't know," he said.

"That's my point. You can't be a real don if nobody wants your job when you retire."

"All I can say is it's because of you Potter Aucoin is dead. And justice hasn't been satisfied. You see that, don't you?"

"No. I'm very sorry if my business dealings resulted in a death. But you can't put it on me. I don't even go out anymore, except maybe if some friends ask me out for a meal. I'm a lonely old man. And now my son is dead, too. It's been a very bad month." And with that he bowed his head and wept.

Tubby didn't know what to say. He waited until Caponata had composed himself and had dried his eyes with a napkin.

"Leo Caspar meant a lot to me," Caponata continued. "I won't tell you the whole story because it's none of your business. Leo had a hard time. His father was no fucking good. He cared nothing for his children. He died in the Atlanta Federal Penitentiary." Caponata closed his eyes in satisfaction when he said that. "So I took them in like I was their father. We were as close as pizza and pie."

Neither man spoke for a moment.

Caponata sipped his coffee.

"So too bad about your friend," the old man said quietly, setting his cup deliberately on its saucer. "But the score is settled."

The rush of relief Tubby experienced was almost overpowering. Caponata apparently was willing to forget all about the Dubonnets, young and old. His brain said get up and leave, but some other, uninvited internal voice insisted he stay and finish the job.

"It's more tied than settled," he said. "Something more is owed."

"Now you're pushing me," Caponata growled. "Why should I do anything for you?"

"Because if the law can't get you for murder, I guess I can still kill your deal. The public might like to know that the mafia runs New Orleans gambling, just like everybody thought."

"Nuts," Caponata exploded. "I'm not into gambling. I'm into real estate. The only Italian thing about the guys who operate casinos is their suits. They want nothing to do with men like me. I'm bad for profits."

"Okay, well, real estate then," Tubby said. "I bet the ground out there is saturated with the kind of stuff that melts concrete. What would an environmental Phase Two tell us about your grand casino parking lot? Don't you think that might raise some eyebrows during your licensing process?"

"It might cause some delay," Caponata conceded. "But inspectors are a dime a dozen. And lawyers ain't much more," he added menacingly.

Tubby took a wild shot. "Maybe you're right," he said. "But what about Nicole Normande? You've kept her a secret, haven't you? You don't want her being known as the mob boss's adopted daughter. Why, she'd lose her job at the casino. Her whole career would be shot. She'd be dragged down in the hole with you."

Caponata's face had gone white, like a boiled potato.

"How did you find that out?"

"You just told me," Tubby said. "The biggest worry I'd have if I were you," he continued, "is that whoever killed Leo might find out that you have another weak spot. If the police get involved, I'm sure her relationship to you won't escape their attention."

"Mr. Dubonnet," Caponata broke in, "what would it take to make you go back to your nice office with a view and leave an old man to grieve in peace?"

"Bayou Disposal off the map. Gone. All shut up. A total cleanup of whatever it has managed to do in a month down in Plaquemines Parish. Make those crawfish well. And also a nice contribution to Save Our River, which is an environmental group you may not have heard of. Think about an endowment for environmental research to the Louisiana university of your choice, funded by the casino. What great public relations. I don't guess there's anything you can do about the five hundred years of crap on the levee that's any better than paving it over for a parking lot, so I'd say go ahead and build the damn thing."

"All of a sudden you don't seem too concerned about your client, Casino Mall Grandé."

"Of course I'm concerned. But Napoleon Avenue is the best of the three available sites according to you."

"Actually, it really is."

"I've told Jake LaBreau what I know about the place, and, thanks to Leo, he knows who is behind the project. His board of di-

rectors will do what they want with the information. I'm not allowed to sic the government on my own client. I might like to, but
the rules of my profession won't permit it."

"Oh. I'm always surprised to meet someone who cares about
the rules. Is that all?"

"No. Clear the name of the dead for me. Potter wasn't using
drugs. Someone planted cocaine in his shop just to send the police
sniffing in the wrong direction, right?"

"That's a good deduction."

"Someone named Broussard?"

Caponata shrugged.

"Right, and he was killed just to keep him quiet. There's no fu-
ture in working for you, is there?"

Caponata's face went hard again.

"Are you finished?" he asked.

"No, I'm not. A man named Charlie Van Dyne was killed over
drugs. Because of that, people are trying to hurt a woman I care
about. I want that stopped."

"I've heard of Van Dyne but he didn't work for me. Regardless
of what you may think, I have nothing to do with drugs."

"You know who Van Dyne did work for, don't you? You can get
them to stop harassing a lady named Tania Thompson. You can do
that, can't you?"

"I probably can."

"Then case closed."

"You know, Mr. Dubonnet," Caponata said when Tubby stood
up to leave, "I see you understand the value of family."

"I guess I do," Tubby said.

"That must be because you have three daughters of your own."

Tubby blanched and turned away quickly so that Caponata
would not see that he had gotten the reaction he wanted.

When the front door closed behind him, he exhaled.

• • •

CHERRYLYNN WAS WAITING OUTSIDE IN THE CORVAIR, and Tubby asked her to drive.

"Go to Friday's or someplace," he said, "and I'll buy you a sandwich."

When they got a table he ordered a Diet Barq's to show her he was reforming. She, on the other hand, ordered a White Russian, and then a refill, while she went on merrily about what a nice street Joe Caponata lived on.

Tubby finally broke in.

"Do you know what this is all about?" he demanded.

"What?" she asked, startled.

"The deal I cut with that old bastard you're so fond of."

"No. You didn't tell me."

"Well, I just cheated the legal system." He gestured dangerously. "I forgave murders and passed out sentences like I hold the scales of justice in my hand."

"I'm not really sure what you're talking about, Mr. Dubonnet," Cherrylynn said with a worried expression.

"No, of course not," Tubby said, collecting himself.

"You must miss having Mr. Turntide around," she said after a moment. "I know it would help you a lot to have another lawyer to talk with."

Tubby shuddered. He didn't like to think about his ex-partner. He took a deep breath and tried to relax.

"You do just fine to talk to," he told Cherrylynn.

She blushed.

"I don't know the ins and outs like you do, boss," she said. "To me, Joe Caponata is just some colorful old-timer like Pete Fountain or Nash Roberts."

"He's a rat."

"I'm sure he is. But did you see all the mandevilla he had blooming on the fence in his front yard? I thought it was so beautiful. He must spend a lot of time with his plants."

"Yeah," Tubby said. He swallowed the last of his root beer. Someday I'll be just another New Orleans old-timer, too, he thought. I'll plant a beautiful garden, support the church, and go to Saints games, and all will be forgiven. God, it's hard not to love this city. It's so ready to accept you.

"Me too," Cherrylynn said, about what he didn't know.

They left shoulder to shoulder, like pizza and pie.

CHAPTER

Thirty-Six

IT TOOK TWINK A WHILE TO DIGEST THE INFORMATION that there would be no lawsuit against Bayou Disposal, at least not until they had given the company time to clean up its own act voluntarily. Tubby assured Twink that the company would do just that, and when he mentioned the gift to the environmental clinic, Twink saw the wisdom in patience. Debbie, sitting quietly in the dusty corner of the Save Our River office, took her lead from Twink, and when he expressed satisfaction with Tubby's work, she was visibly relieved.

"But we can't stop here," Twink said. "There are two or three other solid complaints in that file, and we have to follow up on every one of them."

"You'll still look into those, won't you?" Debbie asked.

"Absolutely," Tubby said. "If we can catch some bad guys, we'll sure sue them." He meant it. When you undertake a pro bono case, you should at least deliver a lawsuit.

When the meeting was over, and Debbie and Tubby were walking across the Tulane campus, scattering squirrels, toward Tubby's car, Debbie said, "I'm not completely clear, Daddy, how you got Bayou Disposal to agree to a monitored cleanup of the crawfish ponds and all those marshes."

"Just the Dubonnet gift for gab," he said. "You inherited some of that."

"I don't know what you mean." She laughed.

They stopped and watched a women's soccer team race a red-and-white ball up and down the quad.

"Great exercise," Tubby commented. "I never had the endurance for it."

"You're holding up pretty well," his daughter said. "Me and Christine are trying to organize a family dinner next weekend."

"Who's invited?"

"You, and Mom. And Marcos. I'm going to have it at my apartment."

"What about Collette?"

"I called her. She said she might be busy. But you know she'll come."

"Sure. Okay. You know I like to see everybody together. But I don't know about having dinner with your mother. We've got our own lives now, after all."

"That doesn't mean you can't sit down at the same table, does it?"

"No, I guess not. Just don't get any ideas."

"Don't worry about that. Besides, I think Mom may have some news."

"Really? What?"

"I don't know." Debbie started walking.

"Come on, what news?" He was dying of curiosity. "Does she have a boyfriend I haven't heard about?"

"I can't tell you." Debbie laughed. "You'll have to come to dinner."

"Well, I'll have to check my calendar first," he said. But he knew he would go.

CHAPTER

Thirty-Seven

TUBBY MET ADRIAN OUTSIDE THE COURTHOUSE AND walked up the steps with him.

"I got a kick out of your parade," he said. "Thanks for all the throws."

"You looked like you were enjoying yourself, Mr. Tubby."

"Oh yeah. I can still fight for beads. You must lose a lot of weight dancing around in that outfit."

"It's a workout, sure enough, but it's not as bad as some of the other characters. The Moss Man, now, his costume is hot. He has to put ice in his suit just to stay alive." The Moss Man, another parade headliner, was Adrian's idol.

"You talked to your dad about the race for Judge?" Tubby asked.

"Yes, sir."

"Okay, we'll see how it goes."

"Will I have to go on the witness stand?"

"If you do, I want you to tell the truth about what happened, just like you told me."

"Even about how much beer I had to drink?"

"That's not against the law, Adrian. That's your excuse."

He got Adrian seated in the back of the courtroom and went to stand in the district attorney's reception line again. He passed a few pleasantries before his turn came up.

"Good morning, Mr. Dubonnet," Pettibone said when Tubby finally pushed past the other lawyers into the room.

"Good morning, Mr. Pettibone. This is Monster Mudbug's trial day."

"I'm dismissing that case," Pettibone said.

"You are?"

"The guy's got a good job, he's never been in trouble before, and he comes from a good family. He's innocent, it looks like to me. The justice system doesn't exist to make people like that suffer. Just tell him to keep away from motorcycles unless they're his."

"I'll do that."

Pettibone scribbled on the affidavit and handed it to Tubby.

"Just give it to the clerk," he said.

Tubby carried the paperwork through and reported back to Adrian.

"You're off," he said.

Adrian was so relieved that tears came to his eyes.

"You don't know what this means to me, Mr. Tubby," he said. "I was so worried I wouldn't be able to see my kid again. Thank you for everything."

Tubby put his arm around him and walked him outside.

"Sometimes, Adrian," he said, "the system works. It can't screw up all the time."

HE VISITED EDITH AUCOIN AT HER HOME. IT TOOK TIME to explain it all to her, what he knew about the events leading up to Potter's murder and how Potter had tried to save the river. He told her about Bijan Botaswati and Mr. Caponata. He told her he couldn't be absolutely positive about what had happened to Leo Caspar, but he was certain the man had died a horrible death.

"It doesn't make up for Potter," she whispered, and cried softly.

Tubby held her hand on the living room couch.

She found a tissue in her pocket and dabbed at her eyes.

"It does make me feel better to know," she said.

"I'm glad for that," Tubby said.

"I don't really believe in revenge," she said.

Tubby studied the rug.

"But Potter did. He believed in paying the bastards back. He was a real fighter, he was." She smiled sweetly.

Tubby nodded.

"I wonder what I should do with the business," she continued.

"You could try running it," Tubby suggested.

"No." She laughed. "That was Potter's thing. I have absolutely no interest in brokering vegetable oil. And I don't really need the money, as you know. We salted enough away."

"You want to sell your lease?"

"If you think it's worth anything."

"I know a company that might be interested. I'm sure that they would, in fact, pay top dollar. And I think that's what Potter believed it was worth."

"Well, okay if you do, okay if you don't."

"You know, Edith, I thought I might make a little contribution to Tulane in Potter's name."

"Really? That would be nice."

"Yeah, I thought I'd contribute to the environmental law clinic."

"It's funny. I never thought Potter had the slightest interest in the environment until today when you told me about the affidavit he gave. I'm real proud of him for that."

"He was a good man," Tubby said.

"The best," said Edith.

Driving away, Tubby sighed to himself about the $88,000 he was about to donate to Tulane. Easy come, easy go. Money couldn't atone for the things one did in life, he knew. Who was going to forgive him for Leo Caspar? And who was going to forgive him for his old law partner, Reggie Turntide? The sunlight glanced off the strand of beads dangling from his rearview mirror and made a bright shimmering circle on the seat beside him. But they didn't give him an answer.

THE MORNING PAPER REPORTED THAT JOSEPH CAPO-nata, reputed organized crime figure, had been struck and killed by a car while crossing Frenchman Street. Ironically, the Criminal Sheriff of Orleans Parish, Frank Mulé, and several police officials were dining at a nearby restaurant and were among the first to arrive at the scene. Caponata's presence on the normally quiet street was not explained. Police declared the accident a hit-and-run.

TUBBY CALLED TANIA AT WORK. HE HAD TO STAY ON hold for a minute, but then she came on the line.

"I wondered if you might like to have lunch one day."

"Why, of course, Tubby. I'd like that very much."

"I could drive by the bank and pick you up. We could go out to the lake and maybe get some seafood."

"That sounds nice."

"Or even Uptown. Go to The Columns, take a walk in the park. That could be fun."

"That sounds nice, too."

"Or maybe we could just go grab a sandwich at Mr. Mike's bar."

"That sounds best of all."

"Really?"

"It will always have a special meaning for me."

"Did you know I was buying the place?"

"Lovely," she said. "I'll meet you there. I have something to tell you."

• • •

TANIA BROUGHT PASTOR GREEN ALONG WITH HER.
Tubby was surprised, but rose to shake hands when Tania introduced them. Tubby was drinking a beer, and he asked Tania and
the reverend what they would like. Both said tea.

Tubby went over to the bar to ask Larry if they had any while
the newcomers looked around to get the feel of the old place.

"Yeah, sure we got tea," Larry said. He pulled a jar of instant
from under the counter. "I'll bring it to you."

Tubby returned to the table.

"You are Tania's pastor?" he asked Reverend Green.

"Yes," he said. "She practically runs the church."

"That's hardly true, Reverend," Tania said modestly.

The pastor continued. "She has told me about how much help
you have been."

"She's had a hard time. She deserved help," Tubby said, avoiding the compliment.

"I have told the reverend what I told you," Tania said. "About
Charlie Van Dyne."

"I see," Tubby said. "Then you know she may still be in danger.
I've tried to, uh, fix things, but . . ." He didn't continue.

"She and I have prayed about that," Reverend Green said. "We
have discussed her turning herself in to the police."

"Well, that's her decision," Tubby said. "If she wants to, I will
arrange it beforehand and go with her."

"Yes, surely," the pastor said. He looked convinced that he was
about to say something undeniably correct. "But we decided no.
Her family has been harmed in a terrible way and should not have
further pain. What she did was just, and though it may have been
wrong to take the law into her own hands, she has repented. In our
faith, we believe in forgiveness."

"Fine," Tubby said. "I have no problem with this. Why are you telling me, though?"

"Because we want you to have this." He took a blue check from his coat pocket and handed it to Tubby. It was for $5,000, and it was drawn on the account of St. Mary's American Baptist Church.

"We had a fund-raiser at the church to pay for my legal defense," Tania said happily. "We had a bake sale and a raffle for a console TV from Frankie and Johnny's Furniture. Everybody contributed."

"I can't take this," Tubby protested. "What did you tell them it was for?"

"You can take it, Mr. Dubonnet," Reverend Green said. "And we didn't have to tell anybody in the congregation what it was for. They all knew. We all thank you for what you did to put a stop to the torments of Sister Thompson."

Tubby stared at the check.

"There's more good news," Tania said. "Me and Pastor Green are getting married."

Tubby looked at Tania's big grin, then at Pastor Green's hard smile, and he put the blue check into his pocket.

Larry brought the tea.

"WOMEN ARE FICKLE," TUBBY TOLD RAISIN, HOISTING A cold dark beverage high in the air and swallowing deeply. The world had gone from sharp to soft to fuzzy.

"No argument here," Raisin said, absently spinning his green Heineken coaster on the bartop.

"I mean, what's the point?"

"Don't ask me," Raisin said. "I've never even been married."

"You're better off," Tubby said.

"You mean that?" Raisin asked. He flipped the coaster into the air and caught it on the back of his hand.

"No, I guess not. Of course not," Tubby added.

"You got some great daughters out of the deal."

"That's for sure," Tubby said. "But when I see them, sometimes, it hurts to remember how me and Mattie messed things up so bad."

"Well, that was her fault," Raisin said.

"You think so?" Tubby asked.

"Why, sure," Raisin said. "She's crazy."

"Maybe, but I haven't had much luck with anybody else."

They drank in silence for a minute, then Raisin got up and put some money in the jukebox. The voice of Marvin Gaye singing "Sexual Healing" filled the barroom.

"Is that supposed to be some kind of message?" Tubby asked when Raisin got back to his stool.

"No, I just like it. Don't worry, I got Frank Sinatra coming up next."

Tubby ordered them both another drink.

"It's just that women are so damn fickle," he repeated.

"They're not much good, are they?"

"No good at all."

"Thing is, you get fond of 'em."

"That I do," Tubby said, and put a few bills on the bar. "Enough heavy thinking. Let's go play some pool."

"Suits me," Raisin said. "Rack 'em up."

CHAPTER

Thirty-Eight

TUBBY SAW THE FAMILIAR FIGURE CLAD IN HER PINK raincoat sitting on her folding chair down by the jail. He went up to her, shuffling his feet so she wouldn't get caught by surprise again.

"Hi, Miss Pyrene," he said.

"It's the lawyer," she exclaimed, giving him a toothless smile, partly covered by her wrinkled hand.

"You saw Jerome?" he asked.

"Yes, and I was so happy. My prayers were answered. You are a fine young man yourself."

"It was nothing," Tubby said modestly.

"Seeing him again was the most wonderful day of my life."

"I'm glad for you. I hope he straightens up. What are you still waiting here for? You don't have to look for him to come out that door anymore."

"This place suits me now," she said. "Nobody bothers me, and the business is pretty good. And I'm here to watch when they take all those young men in. Some of 'em I know from when they were babies. I wave at them even if they don't see. And I like to think I'll be here when they get out."

"I'm sure that means a lot to them," Tubby said. He asked if he could have two pralines.

He searched in his pants pocket for his wallet, and his fingers encountered the strand of beads he had found on Bourbon Street. How had they gotten there?

"You want some beads?" he asked, showing them to her.

"They're pretty nice," she said, and took them into her palm where she could inspect them.

"Yes, I believe I will keep them." She looked up and her eyes, to him, seemed wise and kind. "You're all right for a lawyer," she said.

"Thank you very much." It gave him a peaceful feeling to hear that.

"You sure seem to love my candy," she said.

"Yeah, I like all the nuts," he replied.

The pink arms flew up. Her hands covered her mouth as she laughed.

He joined in.